THYRA

ANNE R BAILEY

Edited by
VANESSA RICCI-THODE

Inkblot Press

For my Family

ALSO BY ANNE R BAILEY

Forgotten Women of History Series

Joan

Fortuna's Queen

Thyra

Royal Court Series

The Lady Carey

The Lady's Crown

The Lady's Ambition

Other

The Stars Above

You can also follow the author at: www.inkblotpressco.com

They would claim that on the day she was born, the Norns in their hall below Yggdrasil smiled, for they knew her destiny.

But it would be years before she even heard of the Norse Gods.

1

———

Thyra crouched down under the eaves, her ear pressed to the boards. Her father, King Ecbert, was reprimanding Edgar for roughhousing, saying he would send him to bed without dinner.

Edgar said nothing in his defense.

She breathed a sigh of relief, knowing that her brother had not given her up. After all she had been there as well, wrestling with the others. In that moment, she lost her grip on the beam. There was a loud creak as she steadied herself, and she said a silent prayer that she had gone unnoticed.

Edgar left the chamber, and she waited for her chance to climb down to rejoin her eleven siblings.

Growing up around so many brothers and sisters would make anyone half-wild, and Thyra was proof of that.

"Daughter, I know you are there. Come and face me."

Biting the inside of her cheek, she did as she was ordered. She faced her father with her hands clenched at her sides, as though he was not a king anointed by holy oil. His imposing figure towered over her, but she did not waver under his gaze as she waited for him to speak, ready to face any accusation.

"If you are going to spy, then you might as well become better at it," he said, walking around his large oak table and taking a seat at his chair. "I don't need to ask and I know you would even deny it. I know you must have been there. Maybe you even took part in the fighting. It is not becoming behavior for a princess, and even less for my daughter."

"But, Father, it is unfair that you would think that," she said, her face fighting to remain devoid of all emotion. "Yes, I was listening, but I was merely curious about what was being said."

"Ah, but that gives you away. You should have had the patience to wait and hear what your brother had to say. Your impatience and lack of trust gave you away."

"If I hadn't made a sound, then you would never have known," she said.

He shrugged. "That is the risk you take. So either become a better spy or don't spy at all. I shall talk to your mother and she shall arrange a punishment for you."

"Father..." But one look from him silenced her complaints. It was useless to argue. He could order one of his guards to throw her out into the streets if he wanted to; that was his prerogative.

They were both headstrong and stubborn. Once her father decided something, he would not be moved.

She wanted to stomp her feet in frustration but resisted the childish impulse.

"May I be excused, then?"

"Yes, and try to remember to stay out of trouble."

Thyra walked out of the room. Her father's steward brushed past her with a knowing look of disapproval. Despite being only ten years old, she had gained a reputation for being a mischievous troublemaker. It wasn't her fault there was nothing much to do, and most things were forbidden to her.

She wasn't like her sister Aewyn, who loved to sit in front of the loom, weaving intricate tapestries all day long. Nor did she find solace in praying like her brother Ambrose.

So when she wasn't running around with other children or escaping her chores, there was little for her to do.

Years ago, her father had hired Father Alfred to act as the court tutor. She enjoyed listening to him, but his focus was on her brothers. He intrigued her because he was a serious man who did not look like a priest at all. When she had asked Edgar, he claimed it was because he was actually a retired soldier who had lost his family while he was away at war. He had returned broken in body and spirit, and it was the church that helped him find some purpose. He must be over forty years old now.

Thyra could never bring herself to ask him if this was true.

If he fought in the war, then it was a war of her

3

father's making. How did he feel serving the children of the man responsible for so much suffering in his life? She dared not ask, not out of lack of bravery but out of fear of the guilt she would feel. She preferred to think that he was forced into the church by an uncle who wished to inherit, even though he had always trained to be a soldier.

She heard a lot of talk about duty all her life, but she never understood it.

Her mother always claimed it was her duty to be a dutiful daughter to her father, just as it was a soldier's duty to die defending his country. To Thyra, that just sounded like a nice way of saying sacrifice yourself. Did she not deserve to be happy?

Thyra was sure she was steaming like the dragons who breathed fire in Father Alfred's tales. For the rest of the day, she avoided her mother's room like it carried the plague.

She snuck to the kitchen, where one of the kitchen maids who liked her gave her a tiny pastry filled with freshly picked wild berries.

"Don't go telling everyone I'm handing these out to you, or I'll get in trouble for sure."

"I won't," she said, knowing she would be a fool to do so.

Outside the hot kitchen, Thyra was ready to take a bite out of the pastry, smelling the sweet aroma and buttery crust. Her mouth watered, but she stopped, unable to take a bite.

She walked to Edgar's room and tapped on the closed door.

"It's me," she said, trying to be quiet.

"What do you want?"

Feeling gracious, she ignored the annoyance in his tone. "I brought you something. Crack the door open."

"Father has sent me to my rooms as punishment. Without dinner."

"I know, and I'm not asking you to come out. There's no rule against opening the door." She hated that he was always such a stickler for the rules, but she could always use that against him.

"You were listening, then, or does everyone know by now?"

"Yes, I was listening, and he caught me too. Will you open up?"

"Fine."

The door creaked as it opened. She could make out half her brother's face, but it was enough to see he had a bruise on his eye. He crouched down to hear what she was saying better. Even though Edgar was a year younger than her, he was already taller.

"That looks painful," she said, unable to stop herself from commenting.

"Is that what you came here for? To gawk at me?"

She held out the pastry to him. "For you."

"You stole it?"

"No, I did not. If you don't want it, I am more than happy to eat it."

It was snatched out of her hand before she could utter another word.

"You are welcome."

She was rewarded by him rolling his eyes.

"Well, what I wanted to say was thanks for not telling on me," she said.

He nodded. "Wouldn't have helped me anyway. Besides, Father honors loyalty above tattletales."

"Fair. Anyway, I appreciate it. Too bad I got caught. Mother will be punishing me. I'd much rather be sent to my room without dinner too," Thyra said, then paused as she thought she heard footsteps coming down the hall.

"I better go. See you tomorrow." She went off at a run, kicking the edge of her long gown. She hated how it made moving hard, but she took it as a challenge, for she much preferred her dainty slippers over the shoes her brothers wore.

As the family and all their attendants and visitors gathered in the great hall for dinner, Thyra could no longer escape her mother.

When she spotted Thyra slinking behind her seated sisters, her mother locked eyes on her and with one finger beckoned her over.

Thyra gulped, embarrassed that so many would be witness to the reprimand her mother would give her. She slunk up to the raised dais where her mother was sitting beside her father. He was too busy with his dinner and the conversation with his marshal to pay attention to her.

"Good evening, Mother," Thyra said, trying to keep her eyes down. Her mother hated what she perceived as a challenge. Anything less than total obedience would cause her anger.

"I have heard that you have been sticking your nose where it doesn't belong," her mother, Queen Matilda, said, not even bothering to look at her. "Well, I have decided that for the rest of the week you shall employ yourself in a useful fashion and work with the spinners carding wool."

"Mother, no, please. I'll muck out the stalls in the stables," Thyra said, unable to keep herself from complaining. She cringed at how whiny she sounded, but she couldn't help it. Working at the loom was terribly boring. The minutes seemed to drag on and her fingers hurt after. Carding wool was even worse. The monotony of dragging the handcarders over and over through the wool would seem endless.

Her mother didn't have to say anything; she just turned her head slowly, her eyes burning with fury. Thyra was quick to apologize.

"As you wish, Mother."

"Good. This shouldn't even be seen as a punishment. It is a useful skill you should be applying yourself to. I never had this problem with your other sisters."

"I know. I will do my best," Thyra said, deciding it was best not to argue. Her oldest sister, Emma, was the only one who truly enjoyed this type of work, or Aewyn with her tapestries. She shuddered, unable to imagine herself becoming like them.

She was dismissed without another word from her

mother. Father Alfred spared her a glance, but he did not offer her any consolation.

That night, Thyra fell asleep dreading the morning. Already it felt like her hands ached.

She wished to be out riding with her brothers or chasing the geese around the outer moat. If it was warm enough, she bet the other children would swim in the pond while she would be stuck inside.

This was why she loved the blissful obscurity that came with being one of the middle children. She was neither young enough for the nursemaids to fuss over nor old enough that her father and mother would be trying to plan her future.

In truth, there were so many of them, she wondered how in the world her parents would find places for all of them.

In the morning, she dragged her feet to the women's quarters, wearing a grim expression. Thyra had been tempted to not go, but she knew that eventually her mother would discover that she did not do as she was told. She appeared in her mother's antechamber where women gathered, all working on one project or another.

Her sister Aewyn was there, working with the help of a chambermaid on a tapestry she had begun over a year ago. Its bright threads were the envy of everyone. Her father had said it would become a part of her dowry when she got married one day.

"Thyra, you are late as usual," Aewyn said when she noticed her at last.

"I was not told I should arrive at a certain time," Thyra said, quick to snap back.

Aewyn's doe eyes narrowed. She couldn't maintain her composure for long. Thyra knew she loved acting like one of the famous ladies in ballads, but she was just as fiery as the rest of their father's brood.

"You shall sit with Maud over there by the window. Carding wool should be something you could handle."

Thyra fought the urge to say something harsh in return. She stalked off, her head held high.

She wouldn't admit it, but at least she could sit while carding the wool. It was boring and often her mind wandered, but she didn't know how the other women stood on their feet for hours on end.

Maud didn't say a word to her as she handed her a pair of brushes with sharp bristles. She would run a lump of wool through them. There were baskets upon baskets of wool to work through.

She knew she could never finish all of this today and have a chance to escape.

Some women talked while they worked, but Thyra was not interested in anything they had to say. She was resenting giving her brother that pastry. What a treat it would be now.

Her hands were sore. She was unused to the motion, having always escaped this chore when she was younger.

"Have you done so little after all this time?"

Thyra looked up through drowsy eyes to see Aewyn looking at the basket beside her, a hand reaching down to touch the carded fibers.

9

"I haven't taken a break."

"But you've certainly moved no faster than a snail's pace," Aewyn said, her lips twisted in a sneer.

Thyra wanted to say something but saw the other women watching the exchange. They were just waiting for her to act out. She would bet that she would be in even more trouble if she said anything. So she merely shrugged.

"I'll try to do better, Sister. Not everyone can be as clever with thread as you."

It was satisfying to see her sister's look of surprise. Just because she preferred to ride horses or run around playing all day didn't mean she was dull-witted.

"Well, you may go down to the kitchens if you are hungry," Aewyn said before turning to leave.

Thyra was stubborn and refused to move. Besides, she was worried that her legs had fallen asleep after sitting for so long.

The sun was waning. Only then was she dismissed. The lack of light in the room would strain her eyes unnecessarily, and there was no point in her going blind.

Thyra gobbled up her food, even though her arms were straining with the effort of bringing the spoon to her mouth. Tomorrow they would feel even worse. She knew this from the time she had spent with a practice sword in the courtyard.

Her elder brother had let her have a go, and she practiced with him when no one was around. It would be considered unladylike for her to be taking part in such things. But in this busy court with children running around everywhere, no one would notice if she wore breeches one day and hid her mop of hair under a cap.

Edgar was at dinner too. He seemed to be in a better mood because he spared her a smile and asked where she had been all day. The bruise on his eye had swelled now. It was made even more noticeable because of his pale coloring. Even his hair was so blond it was nearly white.

Thyra envied him that complexion that was so fashionable. Her own dark hair was unremarkable. She did not mind keeping it braided up and hidden beneath a coif.

Her older sisters wore veils held in place by delicate circlets on their head.

She used to envy them this decoration, but now she found her eyes drawn to the intricate hilts of her brothers' swords. Her elder brother, Athelstan, her father's heir, had one with a lion's head carved into it.

After dinner, she crawled into bed, too weary from the long day to think of going to hear Father Alfred's stories or watch some acrobats perform for her father.

She wasn't even awoken by her two other sisters getting into bed either.

She dreamed of having her own bed one day, but the royal family was too large for it to be practical.

As the days went by, Thyra found that it was getting easier. She began challenging herself to get more and more done. It did not matter what she accomplished.

No one was actually checking the quantity of the work done. They just wanted to make sure she was sitting down every day for the allotted hours. Aewyn was always ready with a degrading comment.

But Thyra did not care.

She imagined herself in an empty, silent room with nothing but the wool and the paddles. She worked and worked and waited to be free.

The fourth day, she was resting on the ramparts, watching the sun dip below the horizon.

Soldiers patrolling gave her a wide berth, so she could actually enjoy the peace and quiet of the evening with a chunk of cheese and bread tied in a cloth. She was finishing the last of it and was about to find Edgar to play a game of cards or something when she spotted dust being kicked up by a horse off in the distance.

She squinted.

Thyra was sure she wasn't imagining it now. A small retinue of men were cantering this way in a rush.

For the briefest of moments she hesitated, then called out, "Riders approaching."

The trained men-at-arms turned their attention to her and the direction she was pointing. The captain ordered the gates to be closed, and the men tensed. No visitor that they knew of was due to arrive today.

Thyra smiled as the captain chastised one of the men for not paying attention.

"The princess's eagle eyes may have just saved us from being taken by surprise. What use are you if a little girl has better eyes than you?"

"I am sorry, sir," the man said in response. "Thank you, Princess." He bowed his head to her.

Thyra stood a little straighter, just as her father did in his great hall, except there was a bit of crust in her hand, not a sword.

"You should go inside, Princess," the captain said.

His words were not unkind, and his eyes were fixed on the road, but Thyra's shoulders slumped. There was little she could do, but she would have preferred to be allowed to watch or even greet the visitors.

But someone would have already sent for her father.

She wouldn't be needed.

Her sisters came running up to her as she appeared in the hall.

"Mother's been looking for you," Greta said, her younger sister by three years.

"Where were you?" This was Judith.

She shook off their questions with a shrug of her shoulders.

There was a great tension in the large room. Her father's men numbered below a hundred. If a large band was approaching, this might spell disaster. How rumors had spread. It had probably been a mere thirty minutes since she had spotted the riders, but already speculation had run wild.

What was next? Giants barging through the gates?

She greeted her mother and told her what she knew.

"What were you doing on the ramparts?" Aewyn, at her mother's side, cut in before too long.

"I was having my dinner and enjoying the fresh air. I haven't had the chance to do that lately," Thyra replied with a snide smile. "So I am not surprised you always look so pale."

Her sister's hands flew to her cheeks as though to check, giving away her vanity. Her mother frowned not appreciating her behavior, but she said nothing further.

A manservant came into the hall at a hurried pace. He wore a smile on his face as he made his way over to her.

Since Thyra was standing at her mother's left-hand side, she heard him bend close to whisper, "The king wishes you to know all is well and that friends have arrived."

"Thank you," she said.

Thyra could see her instantly transform and realized for the first time her mother had been worried.

She got to her feet and ordered the servants to bring more food and wine, for they would soon be joined by welcomed guests. She also motioned for a lute player to begin a song.

The tension in the room was gone, replaced with mirth at their own fear and excitement over the visitors, whoever they might be.

Thyra left her mother's side and disappeared among her siblings. Her brothers who weren't old enough to stand by her father's side were smarting from being left behind with the womenfolk.

She rolled her eyes. You would think they would have realized how much more dangerous it was to be here among her mother's sharp reprimands and the cruel taunts that could hurt more than any physical blow.

Then the loud booming sound of her father's voice came drifting in.

The next moment they entered, and all eyes turned to them.

Beside her father walked a heavyset man who seemed to command the attention of the room. He was not as tall as her father, but he was broad and surefooted. It helped that he dressed richly with a heavy fur mantle strapped in place by two huge silver penannular brooches. Even Thyra from the back of the room could make out the tiny gems as they caught the candlelight.

At the very least, this man was a wealthy nobleman.

Behind him followed a small group of his men, intermingled with her father's. They were similarly attired. Many of their faces looked drawn and tired. Only the leader wore a grin on his face and seemed to stand firm on his feet as he took in the hall.

"Allow me to introduce you to my good friend, Jarl Erikson," her father said to the people assembled. "He and his men were blown off course by a storm at sea and found themselves on our shores. We shall make them welcome."

Cheers and greetings went up.

Thyra watched the man put a hand over his heart and nod his appreciation.

His name was familiar, but she couldn't quite remember who he was. He was not an Englishman, that was for sure.

Her father led him over toward them were she stood with her siblings. Her siblings had arranged themselves around her mother. It felt as though they were getting ready to parade into the chapel for Sunday Mass.

"May I introduce my wife, Queen Matilda, and the rest of our children," her father said with a sweep of his hand to indicate them all.

"You've been a busy man, King Ecbert," Erikson said with a laugh.

Thyra glanced at her mother to see her frown slightly at the bawdy jest, but it quickly disappeared and was replaced with her courtly smile.

"You are most welcome into our home. I am sorry to hear of your troubles," she said.

"Ah, I am not, now that I have seen what comforts await us here."

"Sit and eat, you must be weary. I will see that rooms be prepared for you and your companions. Are these all your men, or shall we send food to your camp?"

Thyra caught the amused twinkle in his eye as he fixed his gaze on her mother. He regarded her with more respect after that.

"Lady, these are all the men that I have with me. Many perished in the storm. I swear on Thor, I am not an invading party. I bring no trouble to your shores."

"I would never suggest you would. Nor that you could," she said.

Thyra's eyes went wide at her mother's bold words. All the while her mother was just casually looking up at Erikson.

He seemed to have been taken aback as well, but

after a moment, the booming sound of his laugh filled the great hall and everyone turned to look at them.

Erikson swung an arm around her father's shoulders, clasping him as though they were old friends. "You have an amusing wife."

Her father wore a strained smile, as though he knew this could have gone one of two ways. At his behest, Erikson took a chair on his left-hand side.

They brought out food in great trenchers for him. Smoked meats, breads, and dried fruits.

The rest of the party ate as much as they pleased.

Thyra was among the crowd waiting for the guests to finish eating, anticipating there would be tales and songs and dancing tonight. Merriment was certain to follow a good meal whenever visitors were present.

Much to her dismay, Thyra was sent away with the rest of her siblings considered too young to stay up so late. Her gaze flew to Edgar with a flash of jealousy. He was allowed to stay.

As they said their prayers before bed, they climbed in.

But Thyra could not sleep. Biting jealousy was gnawing at her. What was being said? What was being done?

She had never seen her mother act with such daring. Father Alfred always said she was an exceptional woman who he admired, but she had always thought that was because of her status as the king's wife.

But lo and behold, her mother's sharp tongue could be used to cut down the bravest of warriors.

Beside her, Greta's breathing had slowed, indicating she had fallen asleep. Thyra's heart was still beating fast with excitement. She wanted desperately to see what was going on.

As quietly as she could, she slipped out from beneath the covers, grabbing her soft-soled slippers as she went.

The hallways were quiet, and she plodded along undisturbed down the familiar corridors toward the great hall. As she climbed down the stairs the noise was getting louder, a combination of music and people clamoring to talk over each other.

She pressed herself against a beam to hide as best she could when a servant passed by with an empty trencher.

Realizing it would be too risky to watch from the doorway, she made her way outside. Pushing a few crates together, she climbed up to look through the window slits at the people inside.

Her mother appeared in high spirits while her father and the visitor were applauding the end of a man's tale.

She was still soaking it all in. The strangers' clothing, the pieces of conversation she heard, the cups and drinking horns being passed around. She had seen nothing like this before, or at least not that she remembered.

Usually, the only visitors to her father's halls were other English lords, or they would travel around the kingdom seeing them. This was altogether different. Foreign.

In her living memory, she had only known peace. There had been skirmishes here and there with rebel lords or bands of thieves, but nothing like the raids of the Northmen.

She was so enraptured by what she saw that she did not hear footsteps coming up behind her. Thyra nearly jumped out of her skin when a voice spoke.

"Shouldn't you be in bed?"

Thyra's hand slapped across her own mouth to keep from screaming. She nearly lost her precarious balance on the crate as well, and grabbed on to the window ledge with her free hand to steady herself.

She took in a boy about her age, though taller who was trying hard not to laugh. She didn't quite appreciate this.

"And who are you?" she said, her tone imperious as she straightened to her full height. It helped that the crate made her able to look down upon him.

"I'm part of Erikson's crew," he said. His chest puffed out at his words, showing he thought this was an honor.

"You seem a bit young to be a warrior or a rower," she said, her brows furrowing. "Why haven't you been sent to bed?"

"I can do as I please. I am Erikson's ward."

She waited for more. Was that supposed to impress her? Who was Erikson anyway? She was dying to know but refused to show her ignorance to this stranger.

"I've never seen a princess in her nightcap before," he said. His gaze seemed to take her in as though she was an anomaly. "I heard all they did was play the harp and sing all day in their rooms."

"How do you know I am a princess?" she said.

"I saw you standing among the royal family as I came into the great hall. Am I mistaken?"

Thyra paused. There was no point lying to him. "Well, I am, and not all princesses play music and sing. Some can't even hold a tune." She was thinking of her sister Beatrice, who confounded the best of tutors.

He seemed to consider her words. "It's true I have not seen many princesses. You have already proven to be an exception to the rule."

She couldn't quite make out if that was meant as an insult or not. For a brief moment she turned her attention to the party inside. Her father's figure shook with laughter as an acrobat tumbled to the ground.

"You won't tell anyone you saw me, will you?"

He cocked his head to the side as though considering. "No, I won't."

She breathed a sigh of relief. She jumped down from her box and held out her hand in greeting.

"My name is Thyra."

He clasped hers. "Gorm."

"That's an odd name," she said, unable to stop herself from commenting.

"Why do you say that?"

"I haven't heard anyone with that name before. Is it common in Norway?"

He shook his head. "It is not, but it is in Jutland. I am named after my grandfather, who was a great warrior in his time. One day I will rule it, but I hope to become so renowned throughout the world that everyone will have heard the name Gorm."

Thyra looked at her slippers, realizing her question had been insulting. "Ah, I'm sorry. I didn't mean to insult you. I was just curious."

"No, you were honest. It is true, few have likely heard of the name Gorm before. But if I become a brave warrior and defeat my enemies, not only will I win my place in Valhalla, but my deeds will be sung about throughout the lands. Mothers will name their children after me, hoping that they will grow up and have a great destiny."

Thyra couldn't help but be intrigued by everything he was saying.

"What is Valhalla?"

His eyebrows shot up at her question, but then he seemed to remember something. "I forget we are in a Christian land. Have all your people here forgotten the old gods?"

She shrugged her shoulders. "I cannot speak for them, just myself. I have never heard of them."

"Your god is a jealous one and does not want you to learn of any others. Well, I will tell you. Valhalla is a great hall in Asgard, where the mighty fallen soldiers go. They all eat, drink, and make merry until they all fall asleep and then begin their revelry again. There they wait to fight beside Odin during Ragnarök."

She was looking at him with a hunger to know more in her eyes. His answer had only led to more questions. But realizing she had stayed too long, she kept her questions to herself.

"I see. Well, Gorm, I hope you have your wish and

that one day you will become a famous ruler. I must go now."

"Good night, then," he said.

She looked at him one last time. "You won't tell you saw me tonight?"

"Not a soul."

She flashed him a genuine smile and went running off to her room. Hoping she would not get caught.

So Erikson and his crew were pagans. She had heard of people who didn't worship as they did. They didn't pray to Jesus or say Hail Mary's. They didn't have a Pope in Rome. How peculiar. She wondered if they were all doomed to go to Hell, as her father's priest claimed when he preached.

She was lucky, and no one found out about her late-night adventure.

Lord Erikson, who as it turned out was a famous explorer and ruler of a petty kingdom in the north, would stay until the end of the week while his men worked to repair their ship.

She often saw Gorm wandering her father's halls. Often he was listening at the side of his elders. Thyra did not speak to him alone again.

Once she rode out with her brothers on her little gray pony, and he had joined them. She felt some satisfaction that he saw her keep up with her brothers in a race across an open field.

Despite being small, her pony was more surefooted than her brothers' horses, and she knew the field well and how to avoid the fallen logs and pits.

Thyra hoped she showed Gorm that princesses could certainly do more than sing.

Something else had changed for Thyra and she had not realized it at first, but she was finding herself walking into her mother's room more often than not. She enjoyed watching her in a way she never had before. It was as if for the first time she had noticed how her mother commanded respect, how intelligent she could be.

She wasn't just doing needlework and sitting by the fire listening to gossip. Half the time she was hearing out petitions and requests. Solving the grievances of the common folk the best way she could. She would then share all that she learned with her husband, and if he needed to, he would take further action.

Once a candlemaker had come to complain that a sheriff was extorting too many taxes from the residents of the village and keeping the money for himself. Her father had been furious when he heard. He had ridden out with a large show of force and not only punished the sheriff but the local lord who was taking a cut.

Other times, her mother administered the household. Making sure there was enough food in the larders, planning where the court might travel next and how it might all be arranged. They never stayed long in one place. A few months at most.

Her appearance did not go unnoticed for long.

Late one afternoon, her mother called her over to her side.

"If you will sit in my rooms, you may as well act as my scribe," she said.

"Me?" Thyra said, her mouth gaping in surprise. Usually her mother used a secretary to write down everything or her personal chaplain, Father Pereus.

"Father Alfred tells me you are talented at writing. So I shall have you start keeping records for me while you are here."

Thyra felt her cheeks burn up. A combination of embarrassment and pride welling inside of her. The crackle of a log being placed on the fire reminded her she had not replied.

"It would be an honor," she said.

"Good, I am glad to see you are leaving behind childish games. I hate to see a good mind go to waste," her mother said, placing a hand on her head in a rare sign of affection.

So Thyra divided her time between helping with the wool and her mother's rooms, where her fingertips grew stained with the use of ink. She had parchment and would record who had come to see her mother and for what reason. She also wrote what her mother decided in the margins.

In the evening, her mother would read them over or confer with her father.

Thyra, who had never paid much attention before, was fascinated by what kept the court up and running. Being the ruler of a kingdom was not as easy as it seemed, nor as simple.

She often thought of Erikson and his men and wondered if they had made it home safely. She often thought of what Gorm had told her of the

Norse gods and Valhalla, but she dared not ask anyone.

She wouldn't want people whispering she was becoming a heretic.

She would wait patiently.

It was another year before she would hear anything more about him.

As it turned out, Erikson had approached her father to form an alliance. He had claims up north in Scotland and wished to have her father's support. For his part, Erikson had offered help against all raiders and even land in Scotland, should they succeed.

The alliance would be sealed in marriage. Her father had chosen Sybil, her oldest sister, for the honor.

For Sybil, this was not the marriage she had been hoping to make, and she hated the thought of leaving England, especially when it was to go to what she called a cold, inhospitable place.

Thyra had been witness to many tears in front of her mother by Sybil in her rooms. Her sister had dared not complain in front of her father and the council. It did not matter much what she thought about it. Her mother did her best to comfort her.

"Sybil, think about it rationally. Norway is not some barbaric wasteland, no matter what rumors you have heard. They are a strong people with whom we have deep ties, both in marriage and lineage. You would be treated as an honored princess there and would eventually rule alongside Erikson's son. This is an excellent match. Your father has met Erikson and his son. He would not give you to a brute or simpleton. You will do well in this marriage. Besides, a lot can happen between now and the wedding day. All daughters leave the halls of their fathers one day. There would be no life for you if you stayed here."

Thyra could see her mother's eyes soften as she spoke. She was not an unkind woman, but she operated on a very rational level. Life was a constant barter that one had to make. Compromises were a part of life.

Thyra knew that while her sister had nodded and outwardly tried her best to hide her feelings, she was secretly praying day and night that the engagement would be dissolved. Sybil had never been devoted, but Thyra always found her on her knees in front of the altar in their private chapel, a rosary clutched in her hands.

Thyra thought she would love the adventure of going to live in a strange land. She would love to trade places with Sybil, even though she was too young to do so.

SYBIL'S PRAYERS WERE ANSWERED. The alliance fell through as Erikson faced an uprising in his kingdom and was waging war with his jarls.

Her father was never a patient man to wait around. It seemed he had fixed his attention on Scotland and would not wait to attack. Nor did he have ships to spare to go assist Erikson.

When she heard, Thyra had to bite her lip to keep from exclaiming that she found this dishonorable.

Later, she went to find Father Alfred.

"Father Alfred, in all the stories and songs I have ever heard, keeping your word has always been a virtue many stake their lives on," she said. For once her voice was quiet and unsteady as she spoke. She had to pause, unsure how to go on without criticizing her father openly.

He seemed to understand what she was getting at. "It is a luxury many cannot afford, especially a man in charge of a large realm. There are many things to consider. For example, keeping your word might jeopardize the people you swore you would protect."

"I see," Thyra said, her fingers playing with the sleeve of her gown. "But then why make promises?"

"Why do you think?" He threw the question back at her.

She frowned, thinking hard about it. "I suppose there was every intention of keeping the promise, but maybe... something happened in the meantime?"

Father Alfred nodded his grizzly head. "It is entirely plausible. Life is not as cut and dry as it is in our songs and ballads. It would be easy to tell right and wrong then, but the truth is more complicated than that. Stealing is wrong, but a man might steal to feed his starving family. Later he might repay the theft, but he still committed the crime. You should study philosophy if you wish to learn more."

Her eyes perked up at his words.

"Me? Study the ancient texts?" She wondered if he

could hear her heart pounding in her chest at the excitement of it.

"Why not? Your younger brother is learning Latin. I think you would excel at it too. Ambrose is a most apt learner, too. You can join us after your midday meal."

She gulped down any apprehension she felt. None of her sisters had ever learned. Thyra knew for a fact Aewyn could barely spell her own name. This was not uncommon, however, as most women at court were not even literate.

Her father encouraged all his children to educate themselves, and if Father Alfred was willing, why not?

"I would love to," she said at last.

His smile was warm as he regarded her with something akin to pride.

"You are a clever girl. Never run from knowledge. It is another form of power."

She nodded. "And what about swordplay? Can I learn to wield a sword?"

He laughed at that. "I think that might be forbidden even to you, but if you want to learn, you shall have to ask your father. I would dare not advise you on this. Some cultures allow their women to fight alongside their menfolk, but it is unseemly for a woman in England to wield a sword. Sharpen your mind instead."

She grumbled a complaint under her breath, but he did not hear.

"Very well, Father Alfred, I will come attend your lessons. I must go now. The queen needs me."

He nodded, bowing his head to her as he must, for

she was still a princess.

As Thyra headed to her mother's rooms, she wondered if she asked her father about swordplay what his response would be? She imagined the conversation in her head, and no matter what she said, her father remained unmoved.

She was playing with the nib of her pen when her mother finally looked her way.

"Is something on your mind?"

"It is more of a request that I do not know how to ask."

Her mother set down the book of prayers she was reading through.

"I'm all ears," she said, her gaze fixed on her.

Thyra bit the inside of her cheek to stop herself from blurting out the first thing that came to mind. She decided she should try to be tactful.

"Mother, is it true in some lands they train women to be warriors?" she said at last.

Her mother looked unsurprised by her question. Perhaps she had the power to read minds.

"It is true."

"So why are women in England not trained?"

There was a spattering of laughter around the room at the question. The other ladies around her mother could not hold back their mirth at the question.

"It is a serious question. I think we are just as capable as the men," Thyra said.

Her mother was not joining in the laughter. Warmth replaced the iciness of her stare.

"It is a privilege to sit behind these safe walls while the men go out to fight. We have other tasks to look to, and fighting is not one we should take on."

"But..."

Her mother's hand rose up, stopping her from continuing.

"It is not in God's plan for women to pick up arms. We create life. We care and nurture it. It would be to defy him to do otherwise. That is why we do not sharpen our blades as we sit by the fire. We each have our place in this world. We all must make peace with our lot in life."

Her mother's words had a sense of finality to them. She would not hear a word of argument.

It took all of Thyra's self-control not to lash out at her.

All she ever wanted was the same recognition and glory her father and brothers were able to get. No one sang songs of the work of women, as important as it might be.

Her head hung down low.

"She's always been a wild child, but at least she's been learning," someone from the group of women said.

Thyra hadn't seen who. Her hands clenched into fists. It was not fair.

At least she would have her lessons with Father Alfred, unless someone decided it was ungodly for women to learn.

That night she prayed for adventure. She prayed that she would not end her life as some old woman sitting by her husband's hearth, all but forgotten.

2

———

"*ADVERSUS SOLEM NE LOQUITOR.*" THYRA'S HEAD rested in the crook of her elbow.

"Pardon me? I did not hear what you said, Princess," Father Alfred said. He looked up from his ancient text, pen in hand.

She lifted her head, giving him a rueful smile. Thyra knew he had heard every word. Every perfectly uttered word.

Seven years had passed since she had first walked into the study where Father Alfred had taught her and her two brothers Latin. She had found the challenge exhilarating. It was almost as good as going out hunting. Since she was forbidden from going out on the battlefield, at least she would have this.

The musky tombs of knowledge.

Her brother Ambrose had left to study in Rome among the Pope and his illustrious cardinals. He was due to return home soon after being away for five years.

He would be shocked by how much had changed. She herself could barely contemplate how much had changed.

Her father had been buried over two years ago. He had died of an infected wound. By all accounts he had lived to an old age, rare for a king in such turbulent times, but she had still mourned him.

Her brother Athelstan had ascended to the throne with little trouble. He respected his father's old advisers and was careful not to cause any ripples in the water.

His way would be to maintain the status quo.

Her mother had retired from public life following her father's death. She hoped to enter a monastery as soon as she felt Athelstan was secure on his throne.

Many of her older siblings no longer lived at court. Her two oldest sisters had made grand marriages. Sybil married an English lord in the south of England, but from her letters to her mother she was unhappy.

She wondered if Sybil regretted praying to God to allow her betrothal to Erikson's son to fall through. It was terrible of Thyra to think that. But it taught her to be careful what she wished for.

Aewyn had taken a ship across the sea to marry the younger brother of the French king in an attempt at an alliance of peace with the Franks.

Thyra had not shed a tear at her departure.

Aewyn had always plagued her steps and made her feel unworthy. She did hope her sister would find fulfillment in France. Maybe being an important lady in a foreign court would be everything she hoped.

But in her secret heart, she hoped it would not be so easy at first. Thyra felt a bit of struggle in Aewyn's life would do her good.

She looked down at the text she was translating. Her hand was cramping already. This was the third time she'd attempted it. The cost of parchment she had ruined was quickly adding up.

She would have to do better, or she might never be able to leave this dusty room.

Thyra flexed her fingers; they cracked. At her side Louis scowled at her, disgusted by the sound. She nudged him with her foot under the table but returned her attention to her work.

Father Alfred demanded perfection, and she had always risen to meet his standards. She would show him all his teaching had not been for nothing.

It was different for her now, too. She was no longer the daughter of the king. She was the sister of one. Athelstan had always been responsible and cared for his siblings, but she wondered if he would have their best interest at heart like their father would have.

Where would her life take her? She was no longer a child and would be nineteen soon. She would be content living out her days at her brother's court, but she wanted more. Thyra wanted a place of her own where she wasn't beholden to anyone else.

As far as she knew, she had two choices. She could get married or she could join a nunnery. Neither very appealing to her at the moment. One day she supposed she would like to have children, but that desire for adventure had not abated from her youth.

It remained within her, the tiniest flame kindled in her gut.

The sun was setting as she passed her papers to Father Alfred for examination.

"I will let you know how you did tomorrow," he said.

She could tell he was tired too. She smirked. So, he was human after all.

As she left the study hall, she ran into Edgar as he was strutting about in his new mantle, a gift from their brother.

They had been childhood playmates, but their worlds had taken them in separate directions. He was learning the art of war and had no time to sit with her any more nor indulge her fantastical desires.

It was no longer proper for her to ride out like she was a child. Whenever she did, she would have to have a proper escort and one of her mother's maids to come along with her. It took the fun out of it. Besides, she was always hard-pressed to find a suitable woman to go out riding with her at the crack of dawn.

"Good evening. What have you been up to?" he said, taking in her apron and disheveled hair in one studious glance.

"I was working with Father Alfred. His eyes aren't what they used to be. I was helping him copy down translations."

"Don't let him hear you say that. He might not appreciate it."

"Ah, but he appreciates the truth above all things," she said with a smile. "Where have you been? Showing all the ladies your new clothes?"

Thyra laughed at the hint of red in his cheeks. The blush gave him away. "I'm sure they were all very impressed."

He rolled his eyes and straightened his shirt. "I am to be betrothed soon. They found me an heiress with rich lands and holdings."

"I see, and who is the lucky lady?" Thyra didn't really want to know, but it was clear he was intent on sharing.

"Her name is Elgiva, daughter of the Earl of Southampton. She has another sister with whom her inheritance will be split," he said. There was a hint of pride in his voice.

"Upon her father's death?"

He nodded, seemingly unperturbed by the fact that he would be wishing for his father-in-law's quick demise. She would bet he had already started estimating how long that would take.

"So with one stroke, you will be set to become an earl. Congratulations," she said. If he heard the snideness in her tone, he did not comment on it.

She found it despicable how, after marriage, anything a woman owned became her husband's. After his death, she wouldn't receive anything beyond what his will stipulated. Even her own children were not truly hers. If they were not of age, their wardships would be distributed among those who the king had chosen. It was rare that the mother would be allowed to keep and raise her own children.

It was one of the many things that Thyra had to keep her mouth shut about.

She was glad that she owned nothing herself personally. Everything from the clothes she wore to the food she ate had come first from her father and then from her brother. Her dowry would be only what he decided to give her.

So in this way she would lose nothing upon marriage.

"Well, I hope you will be very happy together," she said.

"You should be getting married too. If you want, I can speak to our brother."

She knew he was trying to be kind, but she didn't need help from him.

"Don't worry about me," Thyra said, searching for some excuse. "I forgot something in my room. I'll see you at dinner."

She turned the opposite way and let him proceed to the great hall alone.

A thought crossed her mind that her brother the king might consult Edgar when choosing her a husband. She grimaced at that. Well, she didn't have to accept anyone. If she truly hated the man, then she would just join a nunnery. She had settled on that a long time ago.

It wouldn't be what she wished for herself, but it was the better alternative.

She still shared her room with her two youngest

sisters, Greta and Beatrice. They had grown, and it was strange for her to see.

Given how large a family they had, it was hard to find suitable partners for everyone and expensive to provide dowries for all the girls.

Thyra knew her own mother had been married when she was younger than Thyra was now, but she would be grateful that she had been allowed to remain at court learning her lessons and perfecting her Latin.

She worked hard, helping in the dairy, working on weaving, and helping her mother with the household accounts.

In her room, she sat on the bed. Maybe dinner could wait. She could always just grab some food from the kitchens and eat in private. She hated the pomp and ceremony.

A weariness settled in her bones, and she felt she was older than her years.

Tomorrow she hoped Father Alfred would be pleased with what she had translated and give her something new to work on.

Louis would leave the schoolroom soon to continue his training as a knight. She had often wondered if her brother would pursue a scholarly life, but of all her brothers, only Ambrose had that calling. The rest were intent on military glory.

Her own glory seemed to lie in attending to domestic matters. This was hard to accept at first, but since she had no other choice. Thyra rolled up her sleeves and got to work. She had always found weaving tedious; however, she discovered she enjoyed preparing dyes.

A maidservant followed behind her as she looked over the shipment of woad brought in. These plants had traveled here all the way from Southampton, where it flourished and the quality of the dye seemed better. She picked through the leaves, finding a few that had gone bad.

They were lying out on the table in large woven baskets.

The plants on top looked fresh, but what about the bottom?

"So, my lady, the full load as expected. We agreed on twenty marks for the batch," the man said.

She frowned, walking around the baskets.

"Not so fast. I must inspect the quality."

He nodded and handed her a leaf to inspect. "See, my lady, this will make a brilliant dye."

Thyra was sure it would, but she gave him a weary smile. She didn't say another word as she picked up a basket and tipped over its contents onto the table.

She looked up at him and saw him looking on in shock as she began riffling through the leaves.

Good. Let him see she meant business, she thought as she turned her attention to the pile in front of her.

"At least one eighth of them have wilted on the journey here, and you expect me to pay full price?"

"My lady, it happens. Most of the crop is fresh."

The man was insistent, but Thyra had haggled

enough to know when she was being taken for a fool. She ran her hand over the leaves.

"I agreed to give you twenty marks for this, but seeing the quality, I can only offer you sixteen marks. I feel it is fair. If you think you can do better somewhere else, then please do not let me keep you. I am not in a rush and will wait for another merchant."

She had to stop herself from smiling as the man went visibly pale.

"I shall speak with my partner," he said and stepped out of the storage room where the woad was laid out.

She continued searching through the baskets, inspecting the product for any further issues.

Even as she heard his approaching footsteps on the beaten floor, she knew what his answer would be.

"We accept your offer, my lady," he said, wringing his cap in his hands.

"Excellent," Thyra said and motioned for her maid to come forth with the purse. "Thank you for doing business."

"A pleasure," he said, bowing.

She could tell he was itching to count the money and ready to get out of there.

Thyra understood they were just trying to make a profit. They weren't crooks—otherwise she would turn them over to her brother's men—but she didn't appreciate being taken advantage of either.

She helped the servants put the leaves back in their baskets and carry them over to another storeroom reserved for such work. Already three huge vats of water were boiling. These plants would have to be processed before they could extract the indigo, but an old batch was ready to go. A few servants took the baskets and began creating the tight woad balls that would be left to ferment in the cellars.

Meanwhile, Thyra turned her attention to the water, waiting for it to bubble consistently before giving the men the signal to proceed, and watched as the woad went in.

She took one of the huge paddles off the wall and began stirring in a figure-eight shape like she had been taught. Two other women trained in dye-making took over the other three cauldrons.

The change was instant. The once clear water was taking on a dark hue. The more she stirred, the darker it became.

Seeing the water bubble, she knew it was time to dye the fibers.

"Bring over the wool," she said as she wiped her forehead, wet from a combination of sweat and condensation.

They brought a basket of carded wool, its fine fibers white and clean.

She grabbed a handful and gently dipped it into the boiling vat before lifting it again. Over and over she did this until the wool took on a deep blue color. It looked almost black, but once it dried the color would lighten.

"This batch is good. Let's proceed," she said over her shoulder.

The others nodded, and they began the arduous process of dying the carded wool. They did it in small batches to ensure the color would penetrate the fibers evenly.

The smell was not the most pleasant thing in the world, but by now Thyra was used to it. Her arms, so used to the work, no longer ached. After she was finished dyeing, she placed the fiber to dry on a plate that was taken away by another servant to wring it out.

They had quite the efficient workshop going. In two or three days, they would have finished dyeing enough wool to outfit all of the court. Some of this wool would be sold to merchants who would ship it off around the world.

English wool was gaining an excellent reputation for being of outstanding quality. It sold especially well in the countries far north, where the winters were harsher than even here in England.

It was late in the evening by the time Thyra emerged from the cellar. She was sure her face was red from the heat, and if her blue fingers were any indication, she needed to wash and change her clothes.

Her leather apron was spattered with dye, both old and new. Luckily her hair was too dark for it to have stained her anyway.

She was yearning for her bed but found her mother knocking on her bedroom door.

"Mother?" Thyra said, trying to wipe her hands clean. Her mother disapproved of messiness.

"I was looking for you," the dowager Queen Matilda said, turning around. Her eyes swept over Thyra and she frowned.

"Your brother wishes to speak to you, but I can see you are not dressed properly."

"Athel—I mean, King Athelstan will surely not mind. He knows what I look like on a daily basis."

She could see her mother's eyes roll.

"If it was just him, I'm sure it would not matter if you were dressed like a peasant girl. I will go and tell him that you are currently indisposed," her mother said with a heavy sigh before disappearing back down the corridor.

The clicking of her cane on the floors echoed in the empty halls, and then Thyra was left in silence to contemplate what her mother had said.

Maybe this was a sign of her mother getting old.

Then, remembering she had left her paring knife in the storeroom, she decided to go retrieve it. Maybe grab some dinner as well. She couldn't trust someone wouldn't nick it for themselves, so she rushed down to retrieve it.

Her braided hair flew behind her as she hurried down the steps.

She rounded the corner and couldn't stop herself from crashing into the lumbering shape of an unknown man.

She bit back a curse as she nearly fell to the floor. His hand had grabbed her shoulder, steadying her back on her feet.

"Pardon me," he said, removing his hand immediately.

"No, this was my fault. I apologize for running into you. I am just rushing to get something," Thyra said, looking up at him. She didn't recognize him. Perhaps, he was a visitor? He looked foreign.

She didn't wait for a reply, just bobbed her head again in apology and continued along her way.

Her knife was resting by the table, half-hidden by the baskets.

As she snuck up into the dining hall, she kept to the back of the hall, creeping along the wall to stay out of sight. At the dais where her father once sat, her brother was now being served by her younger brother pouring him wine and her mother sitting on his left but on a lower seat.

She could no longer claim to be queen of England, though it still felt like she had the power of one.

"What are you doing?"

It was Edgar who had caught her sneaking. "Come, take a seat."

She shook her head, pulling him into an alcove out of sight.

"Look at me. I'm a mess. I don't want to draw attention to myself. Mother had ordered me to change, but all I want is a bit of dinner and some sleep."

He looked at her stained clothes and gave a low whistle. "I can see why. Your face is stained too."

"It is?" Her hands flew to her face. "Oh no, I'll be blue for days."

Edgar was visibly trying hard not to laugh. "You will be like the mighty female warriors of legend, painted blue."

She elbowed him in the chest. "Stop laughing and grab me some food. So I can escape."

"All right, what's a kind brother for anyway?"

"Hurry up," she said, pushing him out of the alcove.

She wished she had worn her veil over her hair now; it would have helped her hide her face. How bad was it? Usually, she managed to keep the dye away from her face. It had always been her fingers that had been the issue. She could hear the mocking gibes of the other women.

Tomorrow she'd escape to Father Alfred's study and wait for the blue dye to fade away.

Edgar appeared with a small wooden plate piled up high with chicken, roasted boar, and bread.

"Thanks," she said, grabbing it from him. The smell of the food was making her mouth water. Her stomach churned and she realized how hungry she truly was.

She ran out of the hall before another soul could notice her.

She walked down the corridors, eating bits of chicken as she went, unable to resist the temptation. She spied movement outside in the courtyard and poked her head out the window to investigate.

There was that man again. He was leading a large chestnut stallion into the stables.

She must have made a sound because he looked up. She hadn't backed away from the window fast enough and she was sure he had seen her, for he raised his hand in greeting.

Thyra disappeared and continued on her way, trying to fight back the mortification. She was often told not to stick her nose where it didn't belong, and this was the perfect example why she shouldn't.

If he was an unimportant visitor to her brother's court or a lord's son seeking employment, then she wouldn't see him. Ideally, he would even be on his way home right now. But she knew she'd never had the best of luck before, and she wouldn't be surprised if she continued embarrassing herself in front of him.

Oh well, she thought as she reached the door to her room. She slipped inside, finding a hot jug of water and freshly washed clothes waiting for her. Her mother's doing, she supposed.

At long last, after a warm meal and a quick wash, she slid under the warm covers, her mind blank as she fell into a deep slumber.

3

_____

THE COURT NEVER STAYED IN ONE PLACE FOR LONG.

The large party of over a hundred attendants, an ever changing amount of visiting lords, and the royal family moved around the country every few months. It was one of the reasons her brother refused to commit to building a more permanent fortress.

Whenever they stayed in London, the ancient Roman city, they stayed in Westminster Abbey, made of white stone. It dominated the cityscape with its imposing form. Ruins of other buildings littered the city, too. They built some buildings on top of them so they had good firm foundations.

She wondered at the ingenuity of the Romans to make cities of stone. They must have had too much time on their hands and power if they could sit still, confident in their iron grip over affairs and taxes.

How did they do it? Thyra wondered. None of the texts on philosophy seemed to give her any indication. If there were records in England, they were destroyed long ago.

"Do you think Ambrose would have seen something in Rome?" she said.

Father Alfred considered her. "Perhaps, but I think they spend more time studying sacred texts there."

"But there's so much to learn from the past. I would never leave the city until I read every last one of them."

He smiled. "Nothing would get done if we were living in the past. We must move forward."

She laid down the quill she had been holding. "Yes, it's ridiculous. Why am I wasting my time studying? It doesn't matter."

He looked at her as though she was a petulant child once again, and it made her smile.

"Don't worry, I remember that knowledge is power," she said. "And I would never trade learning languages for anything else. You know that."

"I haven't been keeping you busy enough if you have time to joke around. When I was learning, I would go to bed with bloodshot eyes that hurt to close. I've been too soft on you," Father Alfred said, shaking his head in dismay.

She grinned. "Don't worry, you give me plenty of work. I'm sure I found a white hair in my brush. I will attribute that to you."

"When you are done with that text, go to see the dowager queen. She summoned you to see her," he said after a moment's recollection.

"What could my mother want from me today?" She

stopped herself from asking more when she saw he was getting ready to chide her for disrespect. "Very well, I shall be a dutiful daughter."

"It was commanded by God that you should. It is one of the commandments."

"Indeed," she said, her eyes wandering over the texts she was reading. She thought it wouldn't be acceptable if she argued with him right now. Plato had some interesting ideas when it came to a child's obedience to their parents.

He seemed to think it was better that they strike out on their own and become better than their parents.

Thyra had not meant to lie to Father Alfred, but work had distracted her in the storeroom. One of her mother's pages had come knocking on the door looking for her.

"I'll be up in just a moment," Thyra had said, but the page had been adamant she let him escort her there now.

"Fine." She threw her apron on the counter.

Her mother was fixing her with one of those disappointed glares of hers that had lost none of its potency over the years. All at once Thyra felt like she was ten years old, being scolded for something.

"You are late," her mother said. She offered her no chair, so Thyra remained standing before her.

"I was working," Thyra said. "I have been keeping busy these last few years."

"I know, but when you are summoned you must come. Or are you saying Father Alfred forgot to tell you to come straight to me?"

"No, he did not forget." Thyra was avoiding making eye contact with her mother. She did not want to get her teacher in trouble.

"Your spots have faded, which is good, but..." Her critical eye was scanning her, zeroing in on her fingers.

Thyra was quick to hide them behind her back. The reaction made her feel like a child more than ever, and she wished she hadn't.

"There was something you wanted to talk to me about?" Thyra said, hoping to distract her.

"There have been developments."

Her words hung in the air. Thyra knew she was trying to imply something but could not determine what that might be.

"Developments?" she parroted back.

"Raids on our shores have increased, and we are looking to make an alliance."

It clicked in Thyra's mind what was happening and why she would be called in. There would be one way to establish an alliance quickly, and that would be one sealed in marriage. Of her sisters, she happened to be next in line to be married. She had hoped to have more time, but all was not lost. She didn't have to accept him. Whoever he was.

"I am to be married, then?" she said, her tone so impassive and cool that even her mother was surprised.

"Yes, that is our hope. Nothing is settled yet, but your

brother wishes you to be introduced," Matilda said after a moment's hesitation.

"That is most peculiar, isn't it? Or does he want to inspect what he is signing up for before agreeing?"

"Thyra! That is very..." She paused, as if searching for the word.

"Crass?" Thyra said, interrupting her mother. "But it's truthful. I was merely curious. After all, I know how a bargain is struck."

"You should have been taught to curb your tongue, not speak Latin," Matilda said with a huff, pulling a shawl over her against some invisible draft.

Thyra could only shrug. She couldn't change the past. But she decided she shouldn't be antagonizing her mother either.

"I promise I will behave like the perfect English princess you expect me to be. But pardon me if I am not giddy with excitement at the prospect of leaving my home. I know it is my duty to marry, but that doesn't mean I shouldn't get to know the details."

She watched her mother's frown lines deepen. "Your brother has done all he can for all of you. We did not expect to lose your father so soon, and with the financial state of the kingdom, we have not enjoyed the stability of full coffers. You must do all you can to further your brother's interest. The hopes of our dynasty lie with him."

"I understand," Thyra said, though in her heart she wondered why her wishes could not be considered equally important.

She supposed it was because she was a survivor at heart. She couldn't see laying down her life for the sake of the crown, but as a princess, that was exactly what was expected of her.

"Well, clean yourself up, put on a nice dress, and escort me to dinner tonight. Your intended will be a guest of honor. He may ask you to dance," her mother said, as though warning her not to refuse.

"Good, and I hope he will. Otherwise I will be very bored." She sniggered at the anger that flooded her mother's face. "I was teasing. But I am glad to know he is able to dance. Does that mean he is not a very old man?"

"Thyra, I swear I will have you whipped," Matilda said, but now she was laughing too. "I hope he is amused by your sense of humor."

"So who is he?"

"I think you can wait a few more hours to find out. If perhaps you had been nicer, I would have told you."

"I'll keep that in mind for the future," Thyra said, and seeing that she was excused, she bobbed a curtsy and left the room.

She really did have to learn how to hold back more.

It would be better if she was subtler and gained some finesse, but after having to compete with eleven siblings, it was hard not to be loud and forward. There was no time for tricks.

She picked out a gown of dark red that, in the dim light of the hall, might nearly look black. It was one of her newer pieces, although all the sisters shared their clothes between them. But this was one of her favorites, as she herself had dyed the fibers that made the gown.

A maid helped plait her hair back and pin the circlet with a veil over her hair. She hoped that whoever he was wouldn't notice the splattering of woad dye on her face. She couldn't bear to think he would think she was clumsy.

At last, she was ready and went to her mother's room.

Matilda appraised her with a quick look before nodding her approval.

"Very well. Let's go, and do remember to be on your best behavior. If not for me, then for poor Athelstan, who has so much on his plate."

"Of course, Lady Mother," Thyra said. It wasn't about impressing her would-be suitor, but she was loath to make a fool of herself in front of the court. They would all surely be watching her. She could just imagine the satisfaction Aewyn would get if gossip reached her that her sister had embarrassed herself somehow.

The hall was livelier than usual. Loud music was being played and fires were built high in the grates. It was then Thyra finally noticed the newcomers to court.

She had been so busy the last few days that she had not noticed.

However, there had not been a banquet until now, so she supposed this was their official welcome to England.

Her mother leaned on her arm as they walked through the center of the room to her brother. Both of them bowed low, Thyra finding it hard to keep her balance while also holding up her mother.

"Rise, dearest sister," the King said.

Up she rose, faster than what might be considered graceful, but she was burning with curiosity to get a better look at her intended.

To her astonishment, it was the very stranger she had run into before. He looked different now, dressed in nicer clothing, his fingers covered in rings.

She couldn't help but frown a little. Unable to erase her displeasure, she hid her face by fixing her gaze to the floor.

She hoped she was giving off the appearance of a demure princess, but she doubted very much it mattered. He had seen her running down the halls, stained from head to toe in dye. He had seen her eating a chicken drumstick while looking out a window.

Definitely not what her mother would consider princess-like behavior.

"This is Gorm, Lord of Jutland," Athelstan said, his voice jolting her out of her thoughts.

"A pleasure to meet you," she said, curtsying but still refusing to meet his eye.

She was invited to sit by his side during the dinner, and she accepted.

From the corner of her eye, she studied him. He seemed to be a young man, not much older than herself. He had a pleasing face, but he was definitely no scholar. Between his physique and the empty scabbard he wore at his side that he kept absentmindedly touching, she could tell he would be a formidable warrior on the battlefield.

She had to stop taking notice of him. It would not matter one way or another. He would not want to marry her, and her brother's alliance would fall through.

It wasn't her fault. If she had been given more warning, perhaps she would have been politer and watched how she acted and behaved.

"You are very quiet," he said.

His accent was thick, which made it hard for her to understand what he was asking. He cleared his throat, repeating himself.

"Pardon me, I have a lot on my mind," Thyra said, unable to think of anything cleverer to say.

"I can imagine. You were always so busy whenever I saw you," Gorm said, dabbing the corner of his mouth with a napkin.

The movement drew her eye to his full lips where they were marred by a thin scar. It cut through his lower lip, ending near his chin. She shuddered to think of a blade ever getting close to her face.

"I try to keep busy," she said, not feeling comfortable enough to divulge anything further. Thyra couldn't be sure if he was mocking her or not. Noticing the awkward silence between them, she offered him a plate of honeyed dates.

"You must try these. They are my favorite." She held out the plate to him.

He held her gaze as he spooned one onto his plate. "I must keep that in mind."

If he was any less handsome, she would have been infuriated by his words and stormed out of the hall.

"Where is Jutland?"

"It is one of the northern countries. I'm sure you've heard tales and songs of the northern invaders. Those are my people," he said, watching for her reaction.

"You are pagans?" Thyra couldn't stop herself from asking, but she had noted the pendant of a hammer that he wore around his neck. "I mean to say, you are not Christian?" She rephrased the question so it wouldn't give offense.

His nod was slow, his blue eyes never leaving hers. It made her fidget in her seat. Why did he have to examine her so closely?

"I heard tales once of Valhalla. Do you worship..." she started asking but couldn't remember the god's name and was racking her brain trying to remember.

"Odin, Freya, Thor. Yes, the Norse gods are my own." He supplied her with the names.

"Ah yes, now I remember," she said, curious about why he suddenly seemed so amused. Was he laughing at her ignorance?

He took a swig from his goblet of wine and continued. "But many that pass through my country have worshipped the Christian god. I have permitted a church to be erected to him."

"Lovely," she said, reaching for her own cup as she hid her face. Was he telling her these things to comfort her if they were to get married? "We have never been taught about pagan... I mean, other religions. It is frowned upon here." She said this in a low conspiratorial voice so only he could hear.

"Your god is a jealous one," he said, reaching for another date. She frowned at this turn of phrase. She had heard it before, but when? She didn't have time to dwell on it because he continued, "But I believe in harmony in my realm. Men may worship as they wish."

"And women?" she couldn't help but counter.

"And women," he said. His smile widened as he regarded her.

Then there was that amused gleam in his eye again. She frowned.

Thyra glanced over him to her mother and brother, who seemed to be deep in conversation. Likely, this was a ruse to give them time to talk.

Gorm, meanwhile, was enjoying his food. By the crook of his smile she got the sense he was pleased with himself. Or maybe amused? At long last she decided to confront him.

"Why are you smiling like that?"

"Like what?" he said, looking down at her.

Her eyes narrowed. "You are either mocking me or..."

"Maybe I am just happy. Enjoying the company."

"No, you look like you know something I do not," she said, finally interpreting his look.

His expression turned sheepish; then he took another drink of wine.

"I know you are here to cement an alliance with the king, but if you dislike me then you can just say so. You caught me at inopportune moments when I ran into you before. I am not usually running around looking like a frightful mess, nor do I spy on people," she said, careful to not let herself be overheard, knowing how rude she must sound.

"I do believe you have a tendency to spy through windows," he said, twirling a fork in his right hand before piercing a roasted carrot. "I have seen you do it on more than one occasion."

His words left her gaping at him. Her mother noticed and gave her a look. She shut her mouth and gave Gorm a glare that she hoped was terrifying.

"What?"

He was not shocked. He simply continued to look amused.

"Once a long time ago, I caught a princess spying through a window at a sumptuous feast," he said, bending his head low to whisper it in her ear.

She was frozen by his words. A rush of feelings and memories pounded through her, but the most predominant was embarrassment. Her cheeks were burning.

"You were the boy with Erikson?"

"Yes," he said, leaning away from her.

"I did not recognize you," she said after a moment's pause. She barely remembered the boy either, but she remembered he had been the one to tell her of Valhalla.

If they were still children at play, she would have kicked him.

"Why didn't you tell me when you saw me?"

"I did not recognize you. I simply remembered

meeting a princess named Thyra a long time ago, spying on the revelry. I just realized who you were when you came into the hall. But it seems I do have the upper hand when it comes to memory."

Now it was her turn to frown.

"I guess I must give you that. I forgot."

"Don't trouble yourself. I'm sure you have met several more important people than myself. Why would you remember me?"

She turned her head fully toward him to take in his expression. It was hard to make out what he was feeling from his words alone. She wondered if he was insulting her, or laughing at her, or what?

He must have seen her stare because he gave her an apologetic smile. "I am a blunt man, but it is better to be honest than deceitful. I don't pretend that I was ever important enough before to be worthy of being remembered."

She contemplated what he said before responding, her eyes returning to her plate. "You are the lord of Jutland. You can hardly be no one."

His chuckle seemed to reverberate in his chest. "Ah, Jutland is a petty kingdom. Our people are not united under one leader like you are here in England. So Jutland is hardly worth anyone's notice."

"And yet you are here. My brother clearly thinks you are someone of importance." She nodded towards the cupbearer behind him. He only served the king and a few of his more distinguished guests.

He grinned. "It pleases me that people here think so

highly of me." He raised his goblet and the cupbearer stepped forward to refill it. Taking another sip, he said, "England has superb wine, but it's not as good as the ones the Franks make."

"It depends on the year. I hear our weather is fouler than the weather they enjoy," Thyra said, unable to stop herself from defending her native country.

"Either way, it's better than what we grow in Jutland. Well, we can't, but we make an ale so good you don't need wine." Gorm's good humor fell away. He seemed to have a faraway look in his eyes. Perhaps, he was homesick.

"Can I ask then why you are here instead of at home then?"

"You do not know?" He raised his eyebrow, surprised.

"I am not kept informed of my brother's doings." She hated admitting that, but if he was going to be blunt with her, then she wouldn't sugarcoat things either.

"Your brother needs help keeping raiders away from his shores. I have the men and the boats he needs."

She met his eyes again. "And what does he have that you need?" The boldness she was feeling evaporated in the span of a second as she realized how that sounded. Heat crept up her collarbone, spreading over her cheeks, but still she did not look away.

The corner of his mouth twitched, but he kept his composure.

"I also need an ally. I have dreams I wish to see accomplished in my lifetime. It is a hard world for people who worship the old gods. I am willing to make sacrifices to gain a seat at the table. We are a small nation, but I wish it would become greater."

She focused on the word *sacrifices*. "Marrying me would be a sacrifice? Perhaps you have someone else you truly love?"

He tossed his head back in a laugh.

Thyra had not wished to draw her mother and brother's attention, but they turned to look at the pair of them. She received small encouraging smiles from both of them.

"You are not like any other English lady I have ever met."

Thyra bit back the retort always ready on her lips, and she was glad she did because he went on.

"It is nothing personal. It would be hard for my people to accept a foreigner as my wife. I think it would also be hard for any stranger to adapt to a new country, with new rules and customs. My life would be simpler if I married someone among my people. My wife, whoever she may be, would have an easier time."

"You seem awfully concerned about your potential wife. Most men I've encountered wouldn't even consider their spouse's discomfort or opinions."

His nod was slow, as though she had just proved his point. "Yes. You see, this is one of the many differences between our nations, or maybe it is the religion you practice."

"If we are about to get into a theological debate, I would like to say that just because some have chosen to twist the words of the Bible to suit their own preferences does not mean that the religion itself is flawed," she said, speaking as quietly as she could.

Thyra dared not let them be overheard. While they might tolerate his pagan ways, an English woman even breathing a word of criticism toward the holy church would be a death sentence. She had witnessed the burning of enough heretics to know that, princess or not, she was heading toward dangerous ground.

Gorm seemed to be aware of her predicament, so he steered the conversation away from such a dangerous topic.

Thyra listened as he told her more about his homeland. He spoke of the weather and how in winter snow fell so heavily they had to shovel their way out of their homes.

"So what do you do all winter?" She couldn't help but be curious.

"It's my favorite time of the year. A respite from the travel and infighting. We build up fires high and tell tales, dance, celebrate, eat, and drink to our heart's content," he said, trying to explain.

"Sounds peaceful."

"Well, I suppose it depends on a good harvest, but people come together in winter and help each other."

"We also try to be charitable. I've gone out with my mother handing out bread to the poor. We do our best," she said, shrugging.

"It is good that you are not comfortable shutting yourself away from the world. It is my belief that those in power need to help those less fortunate. You are able to live a life of luxury, thanks to their hard work." Gorm was looking off into the distance. It sounded as though he was speaking from the heart. It wasn't just something abstract, but from personal experience. Thyra wanted to ask him more, but felt this was not the time.

Their plates were being cleared away and replaced with desserts of baked apples, pies, and other sweets. This feast was beginning to feel more and more like a wedding feast.

Thyra had never stated she would agree to marry this man, but she would let it slide. Even this one encounter made her think that being married to Gorm wouldn't be so bad.

Still, she wasn't a fool. She wasn't about to trade the life she had here for so much unknown.

She was picking at her food now and lost in her thoughts. Gorm, at her side, had been pulled into conversation with her brother until a bard walked into the center of the room with his ornate lute.

He was often hired to sing and tell tales at special occasions. It was an honor to hear him.

She was enraptured as he began his ballad of how her father had risen up to defeat the Scots in the north. She still remembered as a child when he had ridden back home exhausted, but in triumph so great they celebrated for two weeks.

Twas now September, crown'd with fruits and corn.
  For sustenance of ev'ry creature born
  When many English peers of high renown

In council did convene in London Town

After the bard was done, the men in the hall applauded. Out came musicians from the alcoves to strike up a tune.

Those who were brave enough rose to their feet, inviting their ladies to dance. Her mother used to dance with her father but now, a widow she resigned herself to watching others, tapping her foot to the beat.

A cough drew Thyra's attention to her partner beside her. Gorm was looking sheepish again. A half smile spread across his face.

"Would you do me the honor to dance?"

Her first inclination was to refuse him. She didn't want to seem too eager or as though accepting to dance with him meant she accepted marrying him. But over his shoulder her mother, who had overheard him was nodding.

"Yes, of course," Thyra said, taking his offered hand as he helped her to her feet.

This was a fast jig. The footwork required was rapid and especially difficult for the women, who were encumbered by their gowns. Thyra had practiced with a dance master and her sisters, so she did not even blink as Gorm twirled her around and she was required to jump into the air.

Music had always held the ability to transport her, and dancing made her mind blank. All thoughts and worries disappeared. As the dance ended and he led her back to her chair, she realized with some surprise that he had been an able dancer himself. Despite his bulky form, he had been swift and surefooted. Never once had he stepped on her toes, like some of her other partners had in the past, and that was definitely something she could admire.

Her brother claimed the next dance. They had not spoken for quite a while, and he took the time to inquire if she was all right.

"I am well, Athelstan," she said as the dance brought them together again.

"You need not pretend with me. I would rather know now if you are going to be difficult, and maybe I will match him with one of our younger sisters."

She scoffed, but was surprised to find a hint of jealousy had sprung up at the thought.

"I promise you. Unless there is something very wrong with him, I will not make problems for you," she said.

His eyes narrowed at that. "What?"

Internally, she grinned but before she could reply the dance separated them again. She loved causing some mischief and confusion. Let him keep walking on eggshells around her. Let him try to keep her happy. This was the way she could negotiate.

"You will not insult him? Or ruin our alliance? I have your word?" Athelstan said as the song ended.

She bowed low. "I would never dream of it."

He took her at her word and led her back.

Thyra noticed then that Gorm's eyes were following them. Had he also been watching her dance? She didn't have to ask to discover the answer.

"You dance with such energy. If you had the choice, I do not think you would ever leave the dance," he said as she sat back down.

She took a gulp from the refilled wine goblet. Her throat was parched.

"Some might try to compliment me by saying I dance beautifully."

"That would not be the correct word."

"Are you saying I do not? Maybe in your land women are more capable of dancing."

"Ah, I did not realize among your many talents, fishing was one of them," he laughed before continuing. "We cannot compare the stately dances of England to those in Jutland."

Why did he always seem able to make a blush rise out of her? She could feel the heat from her cheeks. She would blame the wine. Thyra set down the goblet and asked for some watered-down ale to be brought to her instead.

She did not speak again. They danced another dance together, but Thyra was feeling self-conscious now and refused a third dance. There were many things she wished, but the primary one right now was the ability to know what he was thinking.

Did he think she was one of those silly flirts throwing herself at him? She hoped not. Ah well, as long as she was not the one to back out of the alliance, her family could not be angry with her.

She snuck a peek at her brother, who was sitting slightly slumped on his throne. He was tired, she could see that clearly, but trying his best to hide it. She pitied him in that moment. She wished she could help him with his troubles, but there was little she could do. That is to say, there was little that she was allowed to do.

The night grew darker, but the feast continued. Finally, she was asked to escort her mother back to her room. Thyra had expected a lecture from her, but instead she got praise.

"You behaved wonderfully tonight," Matilda said. "I was half expecting you to cause a scene."

"Why does everyone seem to think that of me? And if you were so worried, why not have me locked up in a tower somewhere?"

Her mother laughed at her sarcasm. Perhaps the wine had put her in a good mood as well.

"Daughter, you are my child through and through. Stubborn and brave, but you will have to work within your own limitations. It is the way of life. I am glad you are cooperating. I would not send you away to a life you would hate. Remember that many women are not so lucky in having a loving family such as ours," Matilda said as she squeezed her hand.

Her grip was surprisingly firm. Yes, it was true her mother and father had been especially generous when it came to considering who their children should marry, but that did not mean that the outcome had always been happy.

Thyra thought of Aewyn. She had been so happy when she was told that she would be marrying into the French royal family. It was not long before her letters contained only complaints. It was miserable for her being stuck in her husband's fortress, taking care of their child with another on the way. Marriage had not been what she thought it would be.

It had been a lesson for Thyra as well.

4

GORM SEEMED IN NO HURRY TO CONCLUDE THE
business with her brother. Thyra half-expected to be told
to pack her things every morning, but no such order
came.

Perhaps he sensed her apprehension and wished to
wait. Maybe he was negotiating with her brother. She
wasn't sure, but what she was sure of was that they were
being thrown together as often as was possible.

Thyra was no longer wanted in the dye rooms. She
no longer needed to help in the kitchens or mend clothes.
She was expected to join the hunting party every
morning and attend the nighttime revelries.

She knew why. She knew she was being used as bait
for Gorm, but she would take advantage and use it as her
own brief vacation. She always knew, when it came time
for it, she could say no. She was prepared to do it.

Prepared to take sanctuary in an abbey. If she had to
take holy orders, then she would. Even if it meant disap-

pointing her family. Thyra knew this was selfish of her, but she dared not share her private thoughts with anyone. It gave her strength to know she was the mistress of her own destiny. In short, it gave her agency which in turn gave her confidence.

Gorm seemed to like her ease around him. If he knew her inner thoughts, maybe he would think differently.

They were out riding one day, and she had lagged behind. Her horse had thrown its shoe, and she had jumped down and was leading it back toward the area where servants had set up a table with benches for a makeshift picnic for the hunting party.

She heard the sound of hooves approaching.

It was Gorm on his strange steed. Its pelt was a tan color she had never seen before, and its jet-black mane gave it a striking appearance.

"Milady, are you well?" he said, pulling up short. "I noticed you had fallen behind, and then I could not see you."

"You were worried for me?" she said, raising her eyebrow.

"Of course. I told your brother I would check on your whereabouts. He assured me you would not be thrown from your horse, but accidents happen all the time."

Thyra blinked in surprise. "It is merely my horse's shoe. I am afraid the groom did not check him properly this morning," she said with a light shrug. "You need not have concerned yourself."

"May I accompany you back to camp? Or you may ride with me if you wish to rejoin the hunt," he said.

"And what if I ask for your horse instead? You could take mine back to the camp." She expected him to be aghast, but he chuckled.

"If he was better trained, I would gladly offer him to you, but he is half-wild and will only obey me."

Thyra would have rolled her eyes if he didn't look so serious. She looked over the horse he was riding and saw there was some truth in the matter. He was pawing the ground, eager to be on the move. Only Gorm's tight hold of the reins was keeping him in check.

"Very well, you may accompany me," she said at last.

He swung his leg around the horse and jumped down, landing with a thud.

He was not one of those graceful men on horseback.

They walked side by side, neither saying a word until they caught sight of the camp.

Platters of dried fruit, breads, and salted fish were piled on the tables. A few men were starting a fire to roast whatever the hunters caught.

"Shall I leave you here in the care of your people, or would you like my company?"

Thyra was unsure how to answer, but she realized this might be her one chance to ask him more about his pagan gods without anyone overhearing. She was fascinated by stories, and though she could never believe in Valhalla herself, she could not deny herself the chance to hear more.

"You may stay if you wish," she said.

He grinned at her words, and they found a tree to tie their horses to and took a seat on a bench nearby.

She sat as close to him as might be deemed proper, keeping in mind she did not wish for them to be overheard. However, she also didn't want her brother to hear of any untoward behavior on her part. She would be marched down to the altar without any opportunity to protest.

"Tell me more about your gods. Who is Freya? For I have heard her mentioned, but besides her name, I know nothing," Thyra said as she smoothed over her gown.

If he found her questions curious, he did not show it, but supplied her with the answers.

"Freya is a goddess who oversees the field of Fólkvangr. She is the wife of Odin and mother to Thor. She is a great goddess and protector of all, especially women," he began.

"I see," Thyra said, finding some similarities between Mary, mother of God, and her.

"There are many tales about her, but we attribute magic to her as well. So all those fortune-tellers are those favored especially by her. She has a reputation for beauty, pleasure, and finery."

"Oh," Thyra said, realizing that such a person could never be compared to Mary, and feeling a fool for thinking so in the first place. "Who else is there? I know of three gods now: Odin, Thor, and Freya."

"There are hundreds. It would take longer for me to name them than we have time for right now," he said. "But there will be plenty of time later on to get you acquainted with them."

Thyra felt herself freeze at those words. She didn't

like what they implied. Was he so sure she would jump to marry him just because her brother asked it of her?

"When would that be, exactly?" Her tone was icy.

Gorm saw the change in her and paused.

"When we have another chance to speak alone together," he said. "I know how your brother might not approve of me telling you such tales."

"All right," she said but did not let her guard down. Perhaps she had been acting too friendly with him. She had really been trying to be friendly and yet indifferent. Apparently, she had failed at the latter.

"Princess, you need not trouble yourself if you think I would take an unwilling bride. If I choose to marry you, it would be with your consent," he said after she remained silent.

Her eyes snapped back to his face. Anger at his implication that he had not decided if he would have her as his wife made her speak without any filter.

"It is me you have to convince. You would be fortunate indeed if I chose to marry you." Her pride was hurt, and as always, she lashed out without thinking.

"I would be. I would be blessed. I never meant to imply anything else," he said.

Never once did her gaze waver from his. She caught the fact that though he was serious about what he said, he was also amused by something. Thyra was realizing whenever he tried to hide something.

Her eyebrow arched in question. "What?"

Gorm ran a hand through his hair. Maybe from exasperation. She couldn't be sure.

"Well, I am glad to know you haven't rejected me outright," he said, settling on being honest with her. At his words, that sly smile of his appeared on his lips, and she wished she had a way to wipe it away.

"I-I never..." She was saved from replying by the sound of the hunters' horns blowing, announcing their approach. She gave Gorm her fiercest glare and stood up from her seat.

She tried to hide her anger as the rest of the party came riding back.

"You have found my sister, Lord Gorm," called her brother, as he too got off his horse. His hounds followed at his heels, panting. "I hope she did not give you any trouble."

"None at all, Your Highness," Gorm said with a slight bow of deference. "She has been the most charming company. Did you manage to catch that buck?"

"Yes, we did," Athelstan said. "The men are preparing it for the fire as we speak. I am so hungry I could eat the whole thing myself."

Thyra, still fuming, did not want to sit around listening to the pair of them bragging about their exploits. She made some excuse about checking on her horse and left them to talk.

For the rest of the day, she busied herself with helping serve food, helping to clear the table, and keeping the other women of the party company. She was not interested in their gossip, but it was better to be bored than to feel as she did around Gorm.

FOR TWO DAYS, she saw little of him. Thyra had elbowed her way into the kitchens, where she took out her frustrations on the bread dough, punching it down with her fists repeatedly.

"My lord, is there anything you require?"

She heard someone ask this behind her. She wondered who it might be, but already had a sneaking suspicion who it was. She remained determined not to turn around, even though curiosity was bubbling up inside her.

"I wish to have a word with Princess Thyra, if she would do me the honor," the familiar voice replied.

"She is over there," the maid said.

Still, Thyra did not turn around or acknowledge she had heard anything. She went on working the dough, punching down harder than she needed to.

"Lady Thyra?" Gorm was now at her side. She could no longer pretend to have not heard him.

She looked up at last. "Lord Gorm," she said as coolly as she could.

He gave her a smile. "Would you be free to talk for a moment with me?"

Thyra looked around the kitchen, seeing several people around, many openly staring at the pair of them.

"I am busy here, I am afraid," she said, unwilling to give in.

"I can wait. Please, take your time."

She watched incredulous, as he found himself a stool to sit on and leaned against the wall.

She opened her mouth to protest but shrugged and turned back to her work. If his object was to unnerve her, he would not succeed. She finished kneading and shaping the loaf before placing it on the tray where it would rise before being put in the oven. She began on another loaf, relying on her trained eyes to measure out the flour, yeast, salt, and water necessary.

As she worked, she felt his eyes on her, and it was beginning to distract her. Once she was done with this loaf, she took off her apron. Then washing her hands of the flour and scraps of dough, turned to him.

"There is a small herb garden this way, where we may speak. Then I must return to my work," she said. Thyra saw him nod and stand up, stretching.

The small garden was just outside the kitchen. In it grew the most common herbs they used, from thyme to rosemary.

She turned to him now that they were out of sight, her arms crossed underneath her chest as she waited to hear what he had to say.

He held his hands up as if in defeat. "I come in peace."

She snorted. "We were not fighting."

"You were upset with me. For a while, I could not see what I had said to make you so, but then I remembered. So I am sorry. I know you are a proud woman. I never implied that you were here for the taking. Your hand in marriage would be a blessing to any man you choose to marry. Why would you want a haggard man like me?"

Thyra couldn't help softening at his words. She hated that she could be so easily convinced.

"You are hardly a haggard man, and you know it," she said, uncrossing her arms. "But I am glad you know I won't just marry you because I am commanded."

"If you would, you wouldn't be the sort of woman I would want to marry."

It took her a moment to process his words. She was grateful her detached demeanor had not faltered. Yet she couldn't deny that her heart had begun beating faster.

He had taken a step forward, and she had done the same without thinking.

She couldn't back away without looking like she was running away. She met his gaze, ready to make some great claim about the strength of women. She was tired of always being considered weak and pliable just because of her sex.

But there was something in his gaze that stopped her. There was something heated about the way he looked at her, as though he might eat her up. She had seen men look at women that way. Her mouth went dry, her legs felt weak, and she couldn't help but notice the closing gap between them. Who was moving closer—her or him? She surprised herself by wanting him to come even closer. So she did not flinch or protest, not even as he pulled her into his arms with one hand around her waist while the other tilted her chin upward. Her breath hitched at his actions, desire for this strong, cunning man overcoming her sensibilities.

Then his lips met hers.

Her senses were overpowered, his beard brushing against her cheek, the softness of his lips, the smell of the pine trees in the woods —had he gone riding this morning?

A shiver of pleasure coursed through her, and she found herself wanting more than just a kiss.

He pulled away, breaking the spell. She touched her lips with her fingertips, as though not believing what had just happened.

"Apologies, Princess. I have acted like an uncouth barbarian." He bowed. "There is no excuse for my actions, except that emotions overcame me."

"I-I...it is fine. I could have pulled away. I should be getting back. Was there anything else?" she said, trying to hide how breathless she sounded.

"No." He bowed again and was gone.

She busied herself tending to the herb garden, checking for bugs and rot, to give her a chance to gather her wits about her. Thyra couldn't let any sign of what had passed between them show on her face. It would be a scandal, and she would be branded a harlot. One of life's many inequalities.

She was back in the kitchens, enjoying the anonymity it gave her. Someone handed her some flour.

"Thank you," Thyra said, looking up.

"Lord Gorm is very handsome. You are very lucky."

Thyra gave her a look of anger.

"I mean, if you decide to marry him," Marie added, and then a pining, faraway look crossed her face. Perhaps she would jump at the chance to marry him. "The others said he was here earlier did you see him?"

Thyra nodded. "I'm afraid my family has been using him as a messenger."

"He certainly is one of the best messengers you could wish for," Marie said with a wink in her direction.

Thyra got the distinct impression she envied her a lot.

Well, Marie could have him if she wanted him so much. But at the thought she paused. She didn't like that idea much at all.

She turned her attention to her work. She had come down here to escape her family's machinations, not be surrounded by them.

It was late in the evening when she snuck up to her rooms.

When Greta came in, she let her know that their mother had disapproved of her missing dinner.

Thyra shrugged. She didn't care right now about angering her mother. She was more worried about seeing him again. Her emotions were still in turmoil. Her lips still seemed to tingle from his kiss.

She wished she could erase her memories of it. Especially the fact that she had enjoyed it more than she ought to have.

Avoiding him was becoming harder to do, as her mother and brother worked in tandem to see to it that they were often pushed together at mealtimes, for hunts, for dances.

She wanted to yell at them about how obvious they were being. She didn't dislike Gorm. No, in fact, she was sure she liked him a great deal more than she let on. He was funny, he didn't talk to her as if she was a simpleton, and yes, it helped that he was handsome. The battle scars just added to his allure.

She fought herself every step of the way though. She didn't want to get married. Not just yet.

Then it was announced that Lord Gorm would be departing soon.

Her heart clenched at the realization of what must come soon: a formal proposal. She knew it could all be conducted without her, but she knew if her family did not, that Gorm did not operate that way.

She would have to prepare. She walked along the parapets, watching the preparations to pack up the court and depart again. She noted how the baggage train was lined up in an orderly fashion, reminding her of an army of soldiers. An idea struck her then, and she smiled for the first time in days.

Thyra, having a vague idea of his schedule, knew that this early in the day Gorm would be in the stables looking over his stallion. The horse was a tough steed. Despite his small appearance, he was hardy and quick and could outrun most of her brother's horses.

She entered the stables from the side entrance, not trying to grab anyone's attention. It gratified her to find him where she expected him to be. A brush in hand, running his hand over the horse's hide.

He did not look like a fierce warrior in this moment, and it made her smile.

He seemed to sense someone was watching and looked up. She did not duck behind the stable door fast enough.

"Who's there?"

She hated that she had been so silly. She stood up to her full magisterial height and greeted him with a small smile, her hands together in front of her.

"It's just me. I wanted to talk to you," she said.

"Princess, if this is about you not wanting to marry me, then perhaps coming here alone would not have been the best idea," Gorm said and turned back to his work.

"You always act as though you know my thoughts, but for the record you are not always correct," she said with an indignant toss of her head.

He arched his eyebrow but still did not look her way. She walked around to the stall he was in and leaned over the doorway.

"I came to speak to you. I dislike how this whole arrangement was handled. You've called me proud before, and it's true. I definitely am, but I cannot change who I am. I do not wish to lose my freedoms in marriage. If I did not have such a loving family, I would jump at the chance to get married and escape," she said, finding it hard to find the correct words now that it had come to it.

"So you do not wish to marry me. That is fine. Don't imagine my heart is broken."

She frowned at his words.

"Why did you kiss me then, if you felt nothing for me?" she said, her voice a low hiss.

"I am a northern barbarian, remember?" He shot her a grin, but it seemed insincere.

She examined him for a moment, and she realized he was slightly hurt. Her words were not unexpected to him, but he was lying when he said he did not care either way.

"I never said I would reject you if an offer was made to me," she said.

Gorm's eyes shot up, looking her dead in the eye. His hands hesitated in their consistent strokes, and his horse neighed his displeasure.

"Are you being coy, Princess?" he said, a guarded look on his face.

"No, I am being honest. You once said to me that you yourself were honest to a fault. So I owe you the same. I think you are a good sort of man. I cannot pretend I did not enjoy your... company. But you know who I am. I am not the meek sort of woman excited by the prospect of sitting by your hearth darning your socks until I perish of old age. Do you know what you'd be getting if you married me? Because I do not think I will ever change."

He put down his brush and handed her a comb for the horse's mane.

"I would not wish you to change simply to please me. I like you as you are. I think you have a strong personality, and that is something my wife would need," he said.

She stepped inside the stable. The bay stallion eyed

her suspiciously but didn't complain as she began gently detangling his mane, running the comb through it.

They worked side by side like this for what felt like hours. At last, the horse was groomed. His pelt was shining and his mane flowed neatly.

"Why didn't you just have one of the stable boys do this?" she asked as they stepped back to admire him. Gorm was fetching some fresh hay for him.

"How else do you suggest I meet with princesses in secret?"

She swatted his arm.

"I hope you haven't been meeting many. It might make things awkward between us."

He laughed, and the sound drew a smile from her own lips. She decided she would leave him then. Someone was bound to walk in any moment.

"I will see you later, then. I'm sure Athelstan will come up with some sort of excuse," she said, closing the stable gate behind her.

Her heart felt light as she walked up to the main house, clucking at some chickens that had crossed her path.

It was her brother Edgar who she ran into. He looked very pleased with himself.

"Good morning," she said. Not even he dampened her mood.

"So, are you to leave us soon?" he said, falling into step beside her.

She shrugged. "It's not really up to me, is it?"

"You and I both know that no one can force you to do

anything. Anyway, I know the pair of you have been getting quite cozy."

Thyra did not let herself hesitate. If she showed any sign, he would know the truth. "We've been keeping each other company quite often. It is true."

"Do you like him? You know Athelstan likes to play nice, but he won't be above forcing you to marry him. He needs this alliance. He will stop you from trying to escape to a cloister. I wouldn't put it past him to drag you by the hair up to the altar."

That made her stop in her tracks. She faced Edgar and saw nothing to indicate he was being deceitful.

"Athelstan would never do that," she said.

He shook his head. "Believe that if you want, but it is not the truth. I have ridden out with him. I have seen how ruthless he can be, especially when he is desperate. If he can't get this alliance sealed, then his power will be eroded. He needs to show he can defend the coasts, or the nobles will turn from him."

Thyra met her brother's dark eyes, a mirror of her own.

"I like him, but I do not like having my hand forced," she said. They weren't usually honest with each other, but this moment called for it. Their days of playing as children had not been simply washed away now that they moved in different circles.

For all his faults, Edgar was loyal and kind, though he would hate to admit it.

"If you decide you do not wish to marry him, you must let me know soon." He looked around them as he spoke to make sure no one overheard. "I will help you get out."

He turned to go, but she grabbed his hand in hers.

"Why would you do this?" She was frowning. "You would risk our brother's wrath over me?"

Edgar shrugged. "I guess I like stirring up trouble whenever I can. I don't think you deserve to be forced to marry. Besides, you would make Lord Gorm so miserable he would not uphold his end of the bargain. It is just a shame Athelstan doesn't see it that way."

She grinned. "Very true. I would find clever ways to exact my revenge." She paused. "Edgar, thank you. It means a lot to me that you are willing to do this. Even if you have ulterior motives."

He nodded. "Soon, I shall be lord of my own domain and won't have time to stir up trouble at home. So take advantage while you can."

She chuckled. Once he was gone, she continued up to the women's solar, where her mother was sure to be sitting among all the ladies of the court.

She had been a neglectful child of late and wished to spend the day with her.

Matilda was hard at work embroidering the edges of a fine piece of silk cloth. It was stark white, and the black edge embroidery on it looked striking.

"Hello, Mother," she said, taking a seat next to her. "How are you today?"

"I am well," she replied as she nipped a piece of thread between her teeth.

"What are you working on?" she said, running her hand over the beautiful silk. It was cool to the touch.

"A wedding veil."

Thyra felt her blood rush from her face. She knew she must now look as white as the veil. Her mouth was dry, and it took her a moment to gather her courage to say more.

"I have never agreed to anything yet. If it is to be for me."

"Thyra, you have nothing to complain about. I've watched you together. You get along quite nicely. You've been afforded an opportunity many women do not have. I never met your father until our wedding day."

Her mother had that steely look in her eye, knowing she wouldn't hear of any argument.

Sickened, Thyra stood up but knew better than to make a scene in front of so many people. She was halfway out the door when her mother called after her.

"I will send Marguerite to your room before dinner to make sure you look nice."

Thyra merely nodded and marched off.

Fury dogged her steps. Her stomach clenched. This day had come sooner than she expected. She found that she had walked past her room and to the schoolroom.

Father Alfred was not there, but Louis was scribbling away on spare parchment.

The familiar smell of the room soothed her. She picked up one volume of Latin and began reading, getting lost in the words. When her old tutor reappeared in the room, he did not say a word about her sudden appearance. He gave her a nod and sat down to his work.

The sun was dimming, and Louis excused himself.

Thyra remained where she sat. Finding she was not brave enough to face the world just yet.

"Princess Thyra, you should think of heading to dinner. There is to be a great banquet tonight," Father Alfred said.

"I will..." But her voice trailed off.

"You should know that it is easier to accept the things you cannot change. Time will march on regardless of whether you want it to or not," he said.

She knew he was offering her some solace, but it was not her way to just accept things as they were. Thyra set down her book and headed to her room. She hoped Gorm would understand.

Marguerite was there waiting for her, pacing the room while holding on to a hairbrush as though it was a weapon. The relief on her face when she saw Thyra was obvious.

"There you are. The queen dowager would have had my head," she said, rushing forward. "I need to get you ready."

Deciding to be obedient, Thyra sat down on a stool and let her work on braiding her long dark hair. Her hair was thick and heavy and disliked being manipulated. Marguerite had her work cut out for her.

A ruby pendant was placed around her neck. The jewel was one of her mother's. Thyra recognized it as she ran her hands over the heavy chain. Her father had given it to her shortly before his death. The red ruby was supposed to represent her mother's faith and loyalty. Despite the meaning, Thyra treasured the opportunity to wear this.

She would think of her father as she marched off to do what she had to do this night. She would imagine she was on a battlefield, facing down the oncoming army. She would have to remain as firm and as still as he did.

Garlands were strung along the room. Musicians played and people danced. Platters of food were weaving their way through the hall.

This day would double as the May Day celebration. Unmarried women wore their hair uncovered or braided as she had done. Men would offer them flower crowns for their hair. It was a flirtatious ritual that her mother had always frowned upon. It encouraged licentious behavior, but Athelstan seemed to think differently, or at least he did not mind.

Thyra was dressed in a dark green gown, a gold belt around her waist and the jewel around her neck. If she did not know what was coming, she might enjoy this day.

She was pulled into the ring of dancing the moment she arrived. The spirit in the hall was so merry and everyone seemed half-drunk already.

Deciding she might as well have fun, she danced with reckless abandon. A wide smile on her face as she danced with partner after partner.

Someone tapped her shoulder as yet another dance was about to begin. A hand wrapped itself around her waist, spinning her around.

She was face-to-face with Gorm. Her breath hitched.

"Yes?" she said, slightly breathless and trying not to notice how close to each other they were.

"Will you dance with me next?"

She nodded.

"I thought you might say no. Your instinct is always to say no," he said, just before the dance pulled them apart. She moved around the dance floor, her heart beating fast in her chest. She wondered if he could read her mind. Would he feel betrayed when she spoke at last?

Thyra couldn't dwell on what might happen. As the dance picked up the tempo, she decided to focus on the present.

Their arms were locked around each other again. Gorm stepped close. She could rest her head on his chest if she wished to. It was an odd thing to think of.

Then they pulled apart once more.

The music ended with them on opposite sides of the room. He seemed to be approaching her for another dance but someone else had reached her first. As she accepted his request she swore she had seen a flash of anger in Gorm's eyes.

After another three dances, she found herself barely able to stand. She had eaten little today and was light-headed. She couldn't remember the last time she had so much fun.

It was always this way on May Day.

Thyra took the arm Gorm offered her and all but leaned on him as he led her to her brother and mother.

They looked irritated with her but, seeing that Gorm was in good spirits, said nothing to reprimand her.

As they drew closer the room went quiet. Thyra looked around and saw that the musicians had stopped playing and most people were now fixing their attention on the throne. Her brother had stood up, ready to address the crowd. She drew in a breath and said a private prayer.

"Princess Thyra, my sister, today you are being honored above all others" Athelstan began. She didn't even hear everything he was saying. She was looking at Gorm at her side. His face was unreadable. "Lord Gorm has asked for your hand in marriage, and I have given him my consent."

There was no room for her to say anything. So she spoke in the moment he paused to take a breath.

"But I have not given my consent. I have not even been asked," she said. Her voice was steady and clear. She was sure even those at the back of the room could hear her.

Gorm did not move at her words, but she felt him stiffen beside her. She removed her arm from his. She would stand on her own for this. She had a room full of witnesses. If her brother was really so unsure of her, he should have done this privately and had a priest on hand to marry her right then and there.

"Lord Gorm, I am honored by your desire to marry me," she said, turning to face him. Out of the corner of her eye her mother leapt up from her chair, pure anger on her face. "Do you truly wish to marry me?"

"I do, Princess," he said, his voice gruff. He looked almost resigned to her rejecting him so publicly.

"Then I accept, but on one condition," she went on.

His storm-gray eyes met hers. "Name your condition."

"If I am to marry you, you must become a king. You must unite your nation under your banner. Then I will come to you with open arms."

"Thyra!" her mother all but shouted from the dais, regardless of court protocol.

Thyra turned away from Gorm for a moment and saw her brother had gone as white as a sheet. Then Gorm's laugh broke the silence that had fallen on the hall.

"If that is all, then of course I accept," he said, a grin on his face as wide as a Cheshire cat's.

Applause filled the hall. Her mother fell back into her seat. Athelstan had recovered some of his coloring and Edgar was laughing too.

Gorm had stepped closer to her. "Then I seal our engagement with this kiss. You are mine and I am yours." His lips descended on hers. Though it did not last as long as the last kiss they'd shared, his teeth caught her bottom lip in a light nip before releasing her. The action both surprised and pleased her.

"Yours," she affirmed in a whisper. His kisses always seemed to leave her speechless. It didn't help that she was surprised he had agreed, and yet she was pleased he had. Gorm snaked an arm around her waist, pulling her toward him as he led her up to her family, now gathered on the dais.

"My kingdom shall be your dowry, and our sons and their descendants shall rule for all eternity," he whispered into her hair as they walked.

She blushed red at the implication. Actually, she was sure she would be tomato red for the rest of her life. Not only had he kissed her in front of all these people, but now he was saying such things to her.

She could admire his certainty. She wished she had even half of it herself.

"I congratulate you, Lord Gorm." Her brother shook his hand before turning to her. "And you, sister."

He leaned down to kiss her cheeks and whispered, "If you ever do that again, I'll have you hanged."

She acted as though she did not hear but plastered a serene smile on her face. "Thank you, brother."

Her mother was no less gentle, squeezing her wrists so hard she thought she could feel her bones rubbing together. Thyra couldn't help but wince.

"This is a good thing," Thyra told her. "Athelstan has his alliance, and I will remain free for a time."

Her mother shook her head. "And in the meantime, your brother may look the fool."

"Only if he continues to act like this wasn't his idea. This could all have been prearranged and this merely a charade played out for our guests' entertainment. If he can't see that, then nothing you can do will ever help him stay on his throne," Thyra said, holding back nothing from Matilda. She was her daughter, after all, and could be no less harsh.

Her mother glared but released her wrists with a smile.

"You are lucky your plan worked," she said at last and kissed her cheek in congratulations. She pulled away to go speak to Athelstan. Thyra guessed she was whispering how he might turn this around to his advantage.

Edgar was next to congratulate her. His words were the most genuine as he wished her well.

"Well, dearest sister, I think you will have won the title for being the mischievous one in the family. Oh, if Father could have seen you now. You shall be a great queen one day, even if it is just one of the north countries."

"They cause England enough trouble. Don't speak of them like that."

He smiled. "I shall remember to pay them my utmost respect in the future."

Thyra was greeted by her other sisters as well. They twittered on about how lucky she was and how brave. Only Beatrice seemed to think she had done a great wrong.

Gorm appeared at her side. His hand grasped hers, giving her a gentle squeeze. "Are you well?"

She was surprised by the contact for a moment, pulling her hand away, but then realized this was now acceptable—even expected. She looked up at him, seeing that he had witnessed enough to make him suspect something was amiss.

"As well as can be expected." She shrugged.

"Too bad you cannot back out of this engagement now." He raised her hand to his lips and placed a light kiss on the back of her hand.

She grinned at his teasing manner. "Too bad for you that you are trapped with me now." She pulled her hand away.

Musicians had begun playing again, and Gorm invited her back out on the dance floor.

The other couples made way for them, giving them precedence.

Thyra felt content. She felt like she had won. It was a strange sensation that she had managed to take control of her destiny. Or maybe, as Gorm always said, this had been predestined in the stars before she was even born.

Gorm and his small retinue did not dally much longer in England. They had already stayed longer than they had initially planned. They left laden with gifts of wool and wheat, so at least they would not be returning empty-handed.

Gorm had even agreed to allow a missionary to accompany them. He was to set up another Christian church on his land.

"So my wife will be comforted in a new land," he had said, while placing a tender kiss on her cheek.

Thyra had batted him away. Lately, he had taken their betrothal as permission from her brother to get closer to her. She liked his attentions but still felt unnerved by them. She had been raised in a different world where affection was hardly doled out. To suddenly be fawned over was... different.

At his departure, Gorm pulled her aside into an alcove. "Thyra, I will return for you as soon as the gods allow. In the meantime, I want you to have this." He slipped something over her arm.

It was his gold armband. It was heavy and large. The braided coils were capped with the heads of dragons.

"Thank you," she said, knowing already how precious this was to him.

"It will ensure my gods watch over you too. With the addition of your Christian god, you shall be the most watched over woman in the world."

She couldn't help but laugh. "Why not put a sword in my hand, then? It might help more than invoking gods to come to my aid."

Gorm nodded. "That is not the worst idea. If you wanted, I would find you a teacher."

Now it was his turn to laugh at her gaping mouth.

She grabbed onto his forearm. "Do you really mean it?" With all seriousness.

"Yes, I do."

"Then I hope you return by the end of the season," she said with fervor. Now she regretted putting such a condition on him.

He had a fiery look in his eyes.

"You'd miss me so much, Princess?" His hand trailed

down the side of her face, his fingertips caressing her as they went.

She wanted to push him away and tell him no, but the sensation had sent goose bumps up her arm. The tingling sensation left her wanting more. She licked her lips.

"No," Thyra said. "I simply can't believe I might be able to get trained in swordplay."

He smiled. "Well, I'll pretend not to be hurt. I hope you can grow to truly love me as your husband."

Thyra looked at him, her expression softening. "I don't hate you, or I'd never have agreed to marry you at all."

He raised an eyebrow at her. "That's a first step, I guess. So you won't mind if I kiss you again?"

Her cheeks were beet red, she was sure of it, but she shook her head. "No, I wouldn't mind."

"Good," he said and didn't wait another moment before pulling her close. Her head tilted up automatically, her lips meeting his. She wrapped her hands around his neck, pulling him ever closer as her lips parted. This felt deliciously sinful. They were interrupted by the sound of approaching steps, and they pulled apart.

Gorm bowed to her, placing one last kiss on the back of her hand.

"Until we meet again, Princess."

"Lord Gorm," she said. Her breath hitched in her throat. She couldn't help but wonder what would have happened if they hadn't been interrupted. She had come across a pair of lovers coupling against a wall. At the time she had been disgusted by their behavior, but now she no longer found it distasteful.

Gorm retreated to the courtyard with his men. His horse had been tacked up in all his fine gear. As always, he was pawing the ground, ready to go.

"Thank you for your wonderful hospitality," Gorm was saying to the assembled farewell party, bowing to King Athelstan in particular. "Until next we meet!" His eyes locked on Thyra before he spurred his horse away.

Thyra, like some lovelorn princess in a tale, would have stayed until the dust he had kicked up with his horse had blown away, but she had duties to attend to. She couldn't waste her time waiting for her betrothed to appear. Besides, she had wanted more time with her books. She had very ambitious projects in mind. Including creating copies of as many of the works as she could.

Athelstan was no longer as warm toward her as he had once been. Whatever tenderness he might have had for her was washed away by her defiance. Luckily for her, his sense of duty would overpower any distaste he had for her.

Her mother was only slightly more forgiving. She scolded her endlessly about how she would have to learn to curb her tongue.

It would be at least a year before Gorm could sail back to England, and she suspected that it would be a very long year indeed.

5

Two years had passed. Around her the world had changed. Thyra's brother Ambrose had returned from Rome, his head full of ideas on how to reform the English Church. In his caravan were many books that Thyra was desperate to get her hands on.

Unfortunately, he thought they would not be suited to a woman.

She had laughed at his words. "Surely anything you can read I may as well. I may not have traveled halfway across the world, but I doubt there's anything in those books I cannot see."

He had not smiled and given in. Instead, he had frowned.

"You have always been wild. You must conform or you will suffer. Learn to be a good Christian woman and you will find salvation."

Her eyebrows furrowed in frustration, but she decided not to argue. It irked her that Ambrose, though only three years older than herself, was acting like he was her superior in every way.

Her brother was saved from one of her choice remarks by Edgar, who had appeared on the scene, eager to greet him as well.

"Brother! You must tell me all about your travels. As you see, I am still trapped at home," Edgar said, swinging an arm around his neck.

Thyra was left to stew in anger on her own, but she knew enough by now to leave things alone. This wasn't a fight she was going to win or even a fight worthy of her time.

She touched the armband around her wrist. It was large and had the tendency to slip off if she wasn't careful. Touching it had become a twofold act. On one hand, it reassured her she had not lost it, and on the other, it reminded her that Gorm was out there. Soon he would come take her away from this place she was starting to dread so much.

Father Alfred had passed away a few months ago, and though the new court chaplain was not opposed to letting her read texts, it was not the same. She had no one to debate with, no one to challenge or teach her new things. She had lost a champion as well as a friend.

She had been in deep mourning for a month following his funeral, and even now, she found she could not easily smile.

It seemed as though fate was truly pulling her away from England, cutting any ties she had with her native land. She often thought of Gorm. She had only received two letters from him. A luxury in itself, she knew. Not only was the distance huge but the cost was immense, so they arrived only with his delegation.

He told her of the country he was building and how he dreamed of her sitting at his side as his queen. That particular part had left her feeling flustered.

At the start of May, there was no delegation from him, and she wondered if anything had happened. She wasn't in love with him, but she knew she had become in love with the idea of marrying him and leaving her current life. She was bored and she knew it.

With a sigh, she went back inside. In her heart, she knew that one day she would be ruling at his side. Otherwise, all this time daydreaming would have been for nothing.

THERE WAS news at long last at the end of June. He was coming.

Edgar had read the letter out loud to her as if she couldn't do it herself.

But the news shocked her.

"It appears your little gamble has paid off. I trust there will be no further complaints or tricks up your sleeves?"

"No, I swear it," she said.

"You've promised me once before, and look how that turned out." Athelstan looked skeptical.

"I was wrong for what I did then," Thyra said,

keeping her head down as though penitent. "But it seems like I was guided by a greater power. For now you are allied to a king and not merely a lord."

He snorted with laughter. Unbecoming of his kingly status, but he agreed.

"Well put, sister. If you had been born a man, I would have made you into a great diplomat. You are dismissed to...pack your bags, I suppose."

Thyra bowed, showing him all the respect she could muster. He had provided for her and defended her all these years; it was the least she could do.

If Thyra had found time passing by slowly before, nothing could compare to this. She found she had no energy to do anything. She could hardly get out of bed.

She had been so excited at the prospect of Gorm coming that she had been unable to sleep the night before. She had tossed and turned to no avail. The next day, though her eyes hurt, she could not sleep either.

Her emotions rolled within her, alternating between excitement and nervousness. She would not only be leaving her home to go to a new land, but she would be leaving as a wife. There were expectations placed on her.

Slowly, the excitement dimmed and left her only with uncertainty.

Gorm had been kind and they seemed to get along well, but that was no guarantee. Besides, how would he act when she was no longer around her family? She had heard and knew of enough tales of beaten wives to know that a happy courtship did not mean a happy marriage.

She felt that she would have been happier not knowing anything. Now she was just a ball of conflicting emotions. There was one thing she knew for certain, and that was that, barring any natural disasters, she would be married soon.

THREE DAYS later she was sick in bed. The stress and anticipation had toppled her healthy constitution. It hadn't helped that she had taken to strolling in the cool evening. Now there really was a reason for her to be bedridden.

Her mother piled thick furs on top of her and kept the fire in her room stoked hot.

Matilda fed her thick broth with her own hands and sat reading prayers by her bedside.

"Daughter, I know what ails you," she said one evening. Thyra was coughing, and her stuffed-up nose made it difficult to breathe. She was constantly tired. "You need to face your own fears and accept it. No one has the power to know the future. Do not try to fight what comes."

Thyra could hear the sense in her mother's words. She would try.

"You are too smart for your own good. That will be your biggest challenge to overcome," Matilda said, handing her a concoction of her own making, boiled chamomile and linden leaves, sweetened with honey. The drink was divine. The effect seemed to be instant, or maybe it was her mother's humor.

She cracked a small smile.

"You are right, as always," she said, her voice hoarse.

"Rest tonight, and hopefully you will be better by the end of the week. Otherwise, your groom will take one look at you and run the other way."

Thyra laughed, despite it hurting her to do so.

Her mother poured her another warm cup of her potion and left her to rest.

Thyra had been surprised by her mother's tenderness, but she supposed her mother was also sad to see her go. One by one she was losing her children. Some were married overseas, some fighting in the army. They were all going their separate ways, finding their places in the world.

She was not a mother herself yet, but she could imagine it was painful to feel left behind.

THERE WAS A LOT TO PREPARE. She had few possessions she needed to worry about, but she wanted to ensure her books and copied-out translations could travel. For this, Edgar supplied her with an oilskin sack that would protect the books against water.

Her sisters had been hard at work embroidering linen for her. She was given a linen shift with rosebuds embroidered painstakingly along the collar and the edge of the sleeves. They also worked on her wedding gown with her.

It was a family affair. Her sisters worked on stitching the hems while she worked on the finer embroidery. She had copied the design from her armband. The dragon's head and hammer. She hoped Gorm would appreciate the little touches she had added. The gown itself was cut from silver cloth that shone in the sunlight. The material had been the most valuable thing she owned, straight from Rome.

Such silk was usually reserved for the highest-ranking royalty, but as her mother reminded her, she was about to become a queen herself.

The thought surprised her.

For now, England had no official queen. Her mother was playing the role for ceremonial purposes, having still not retired to a convent as she had wished to. Now Thyra would be crowned Queen of Jutland, or had Gorm picked another name for his nation?

What would she be required to do? Though the position commanded respect in England, the role did not require much of the woman, except to give the kingdom a son.

Or maybe in Jutland that wasn't important. She smiled at the thought. Such foolishness.

She had to clear her head. Her mother prepared her a large trousseau. Really, she would not be bringing much else to Gorm when she joined hands with him. The items were being ordered or commissioned last-minute. Usually, they would have been gathered slowly over time, but it seemed her mother and brother did not have much faith in Gorm being successful and had not started until now.

Thyra would have felt guilty for the hassle and expense her wedding was causing, but seeing as her brother had not promised a dowry, the very least he could do was make sure she would be outfitted as a proper English princess.

Though his arrival seemed such a long way off, time was flying by. Her mind was constantly on the horizon, imagining his banners flying as he rode up to the gates of London.

THYRA SHIFTED her weight from one foot to another. She had been standing by her brother's side for over thirty minutes now. Unused to the weight of so many jewels and gold chains, she felt constrained.

Only her own excitement and sense of anticipation were keeping her from uttering a word of complaint.

Ever since Gorm and his men were spotted riding up the high road, they had been in a flurry of preparations. Scouts had come to report that his ships had been spotted just off the English coast.

Then a messenger from Gorm himself had arrived, saying that he was on his way.

Her brother had posted outriders, and they had ample time to have warning of his arrival.

"Nervous? What if he's lost an eye?" Edgar whispered in her ear. He was trying to get a rise out of her, but she merely shrugged.

"So what?"

He shook his head in frustration and moved on to her younger sisters, scaring them with stories of northern raiders.

Ever since the alliance with Gorm, the raids had lessened. Maybe soon there would be a generation of children who did not grow up fearing the sea. If she could help make that happen by simply marrying Gorm, then all the better.

Shouts from the battlements announced their coming. The sound of their horses pounding the ground was the confirmation.

Gorm was riding at the helm of his band. Despite his seemingly bulky form, he dismounted his horse with practiced ease. He handed the reins to a squire who had rushed forward.

Thyra watched his every movement, examining him from head to toe. He still had both eyes. He seemed unchanged, except he had an undeniable gravity about him that had not been there the last time he was away.

As Gorm greeted her brother, his eyes found hers. They made eye contact and he gave her a little smile of acknowledgement.

The formal greeting lasted way too long for Thyra's taste, but at long last, they were invited inside the great abbey. Westminster was repurposed from an old Roman building, but little had been kept except for its stone foundation.

It was her brother's grandest home. The city of London itself acted as its fortification.

They were not seated by each other. He was on her brother's left, and she was on the right. Her mother acted as even more of a barricade.

She tried to be indifferent. She tried not to mind, but she kept looking over to the man who would shortly become her husband. Thyra was pleased to find he was looking at her as often as she was at him.

Perhaps it was her sense of pride, but she wanted his attention. She didn't want to have to worry about him running off, having affairs with others. She didn't expect fidelity, but it would be nice...

The feast ended with music, and those who were not yet too drunk went to the dance floor to celebrate Gorm's arrival.

Thyra gladly took his offered hand.

She felt the calluses on his palm, the strength of his arm as he led her. Thyra knew that she would be safe with him. She would be protected.

"It has been a long time, Princess," he said, kissing the back of her hand.

Her wide, genuine smile was returned. "I thought you might come back quicker."

He chuckled. "It's good to know I have such an eager bride."

She fought back her blush. He was always teasing her, but by now she was ready for what came after the wedding ceremony.

"You were such a renowned warrior, I thought you might return before winter," she teased some more.

The dance began, and they were just as often separated as brought together.

"Who knew it would not be an easy feat. I would not have agreed to your conditions."

His smile told her he was also joking. She spun away, her heart light and joyful.

She surprised herself by not feeling apprehensive. She was not naive, but he put her at ease. She could see that they would work well together as husband and wife. Thyra would have nothing to fear from him.

She had seen men like that. Men that had something to prove by taking it out on those who could not defend themselves.

The dance ended and she curtsied low to him.

He led her back to her waiting mother and behaved like the visiting monarch he was and not a lovesick bridegroom.

The days passed by quickly. Gorm could not be away from his newly minted kingdom for so long, and so her wedding day approached faster than she would have anticipated, especially after waiting for two long years.

The Archbishop of Canterbury would perform the ceremony. It would be Christian to please her brother. Gorm had told Thyra that once they were back in Denmark they would have another ceremony where all would attend. This one would be conducted in the old ways. She had been curious to know more, but he had kept silent.

The morning of her wedding, she was bathed in jug after jug of hot water. Her mother rubbed scented oils into her skin while a maid brushed them through her hair. Her thick auburn hair shone, and her skin seemed to glow.

Thyra would have enjoyed this pampering immensely if it wasn't for the nerves building up within her. All she could think about was what would happen after. They were to spend one night here and then leave the very next day. Already her things were packed away in trunks and being loaded onto carts.

This would be her last full day spent in the company of her family.

Yet another part of her leaped at this chance. She had often dreamed of adventure. She would travel across the sea as her brother Ambrose had done and see people of different nations. She couldn't wait.

Her mother seemed to sense her excitement and scolded her lightly.

"It is more common and acceptable for brides to be mournful and crying on their wedding day than elated. What will people think?"

Thyra rolled her eyes and tried to look as miserable as she could muster.

There was no way there had been any funny business going on before this marriage. Gorm had arrived a mere five days before today, and what exactly was supposed to have happened while he was in another country all this time?

"I am sad to be leaving everyone behind," she said at

last, as the veil was being arranged over her. "I shall miss having everyone around me."

"Pray you have many children, as I did, then you shall never feel alone," her mother said.

Thyra had to hide a grimace. Children were precious and a gift from God, but she really couldn't see herself with so many. She would be pregnant every year of her marriage for the next ten years if that was going to be the case. She didn't find that very appealing.

She still remembered how Gorm had said he would get someone to teach her how to fight.

The court was full of visiting noblemen and their wives. They had come to witness her marriage, but mostly for the festivities that happened after.

They decked the halls with candles and decorative garlands. The archbishop was dressed in all the pomp of his station.

Everyone was in their very best.

The ceremony was dull and dragged on for far too long. Thyra's knees ached from kneeling in front of the priest for such a long time. With each sentence, her heart seemed to beat louder in her chest.

This was really happening. Her life would be changed forever, and there was no stopping it or going back now.

At her side, Gorm, who was holding her hand, gave her a light, reassuring squeeze and just like that she didn't want to run anymore. She was steady again.

Each in turn said their vows, and Gorm claimed a kiss in front of the congregation to the acclaim of everyone.

They danced all night, while most people got drunk before the sun had even set. The festive mood put everyone at ease.

As the hall got dim, and the candles burned down, Gorm suggested they retire for the night.

She left first, as custom dictated, and waited in her chambers for Gorm to be escorted to her rooms. As most people were already fast asleep, it was only a small group of men that led the way. Even so, she could hear their bawdy remarks as they came down the hall and felt embarrassed on their behalf. Men could be such fools, especially under the influence of strong ale.

She watched from her seat by the fire as Gorm stepped into the room, locking the door behind him.

He looked over to her with a crooked smile. "Forgive me if it makes you uncomfortable, but they keep threatening to come in to make sure the deed is done. I was not aware this was a custom in your land."

She bit her lip to keep from laughing. "Hopefully, it does not become one. You have probably taken the safest route though."

Silence fell on the room as the merrymakers returned to the hall.

It was Gorm, striding across the room, who broke the silence with a heavy sigh. He was clearly tired. "I hope my men have listened and did not drink too heavily, otherwise our journey home will have to be postponed."

"I guess this is one way to know if you can trust your men. Put them in the way of temptation," she said. Now Thyra found she could not focus on him, and she looked at the fire burning in the grate. She wrapped the robe tight around her.

"Are you cold?" he said.

She looked over and found him sitting on a stool by the bed, pulling off his boots. He had already removed the heavy cloak around his shoulders. No longer did he look like an imposing tower of a man. For the first time, perhaps she could see that he wasn't much older than she was. Perhaps a difference of two or three years. It surprised her to think of how much more he had done and seen than her.

She supposed that she was envious of him.

"It is hard to feel cold in this room. No, I was nervous," she said, being candid.

"Was?"

She gave him a smile. "Uncertainty is never fun. I am about to spend my first night with my husband. Tomorrow I am to leave the land of my birth forever. There is a lot of uncertainty in my life. But I choose this. I wanted this. My nerves disappeared. I realized I would not be doing this alone, but with you."

He seemed to consider her for a moment. Then, carefully, as though approaching a timid cat, he made his way over to her, kneeling at her feet.

"You shall not be alone. I can promise you that."

"But can you promise me never to fall in battle?" she said, her mind wistful as she thought of how many wives were left at home, never to see their husbands again.

He did not answer.

Her fingers wound in his hair and stroked the fine

soft hair in a soothing motion. "I wish I was a fool. Then it might be easy to believe such promises."

He touched the armband around her wrist. "I swear by all the gods that I shall not leave you if I can. It is a great honor among my people to die in battle, but for you, I am willing to die an old man in my bed. I swear it."

She cupped his face in her hands. Thyra was deeply touched. She tried to find any trace of insincerity in his face but could not.

"Thank you," she said as she leaned forward to place a tender kiss on his lips.

He sighed, and it encouraged her to do more than just kiss him. She pulled him closer, her hands winding their way behind his head as she slid herself onto his lap.

His hands roamed over her body as he pulled her close. She let out a groan of pleasure as his hand caressed the back of her neck. With the other, he began hiking her nightshirt up her leg. Goose bumps spread over her skin, both at his touch and from the chill of the night air.

Her lips parted, letting his insistent tongue in. She wasn't sure what she was doing anymore. She had enjoyed his kisses and caresses, but she felt that they were going further than she had any knowledge or confidence about.

Sensing her hesitation, he paused, his hand resting on her now exposed thigh.

"I am... I can stop," he said. He sounded like a man gasping for air. Fighting with himself for control. She yearned for more, already missing his touch. But still a part of her was unsure.

"Don't. But let's get off the floor," she said at last, feeling it was not comfortable.

With one sweeping motion, he picked her off the floor.

"Where to, milady?"

She laughed and pointed to the bed. "You are making me act the part of the needy harlot."

"You? Never. You are my princess," he said, placing a kiss on her neck. He lowered her to the bed, and another kiss on her collarbone that sent shivers down her spine silenced any reply she might make. They didn't speak much after that. Neither letting the other get a word in.

She spent the night in surprising bliss, feeling beautiful and desired. Thyra wasn't sure what she had done to deserve such a loving man.

But she was glad she had not rejected him out of hand.

The early morning light filtered through the room. They had forgotten to shut the blinds. She was up first, a bit sore and unsteady on her feet. Her head pounding from exhaustion and the wine she had drunk.

She threw on her discarded night shift and braided her hair, which was now a matted mess running down her back.

She hoped she looked somewhat presentable. She looked over at Gorm's sleeping form, his bare back exposed to her. The thought struck her that she might climb back into bed, but she stopped. She knew that soon her maids and mother would come knocking, and any desire she felt building quickly dissipated. Besides, they had a journey to prepare for.

With her robe tied tightly around her, she moved back toward him, his clothes gathered in her hands.

"Gorm, wake up," she said, nudging him gently with her free hand.

He did not stir, and she had to poke him harder. Still nothing.

"My love, your fleet was set aflame and you shall be trapped here at my brother's mercy if you do not wake up," she whispered in his ear.

Only a moment passed before he jumped to his feet with a start, to then fall back down on the bed, with a hand to his head. She could not maintain her composure and laughed.

"The ships!"

"Shhh. Your ships are fine. I hope. It's good to know so early in our marriage how best to rouse you," she said, shoving his clothes toward him. "Get dressed. I'm sure we won't be left alone for much longer."

He groaned into his pillow but with a stretch got up.

She tried not to watch him as he dressed. Occasionally, she couldn't help herself.

"And how are you this morning, wife?" he said, coming over to her once he was done and placing a kiss on her brow.

"I am well, husband," she said with a light chuckle. "It sounds so strange to say."

"Well, do you feel any different?"

She shook her head. Thyra didn't feel like sharing

that, though she was sore, she found that he had awakened a hunger within her that she had not known about herself. Her gaze traveled to the bed.

Before any of them could say anything, a knock at the door interrupted them.

It was Gorm who opened it to admit her mother and a party of maids that trailed in.

"I'll excuse myself, ladies," he said with a bow of his head.

Thyra was fussed over all morning as they prepared her for her wedding breakfast. Many were still sleeping off the drink from last night, and it would begin again.

"Are you well?" her mother said as she helped brush her hair.

"Yes, I am," Thyra said, wondering what would have happened if she said she wasn't. It would be too late to do anything about it. In the eyes of God, they were joined together forever, until death.

Her mother finished untangling her hair and called for the small trunk that she had brought into the room.

She opened the lid of the wooden chest and pulled out a fine golden net and circlet.

"For your hair. I thought you might like this. It is must lighter than the ones you usually wear," Matilda said as she began pinning it into place. "You look like a queen."

A light linen fabric went over the top of this and was held together by the golden circlet.

Greta exclaimed over her. "You are so pretty. You

look like those ladies in the stained windows. When can I be married?"

"Not for a few more years," Thyra said, scolding her younger sister. "It's not just about getting pretty new clothes, you know. It is a duty and responsibility. You are too young and silly right now for such thoughts."

Greta huffed, but their mother said that she was right.

"Greta, you shall have to confess to the sin of vanity if you keep on like this," Matilda said.

That made Greta quiet, but Thyra could see her continue to admire her.

The looking glass was brought, and Thyra could see why Greta was so envious. She looked prettier than she ever remembered herself looking. No longer was her hair braided down and framing her face, but the combination of the net and the circlet created a beautiful image.

"It's a shame you don't have a nicer complexion," Matilda said. "You would have been a perfect beauty."

Her mother could always be relied upon for brutal honesty.

"It's all that horseback riding you used to do," Beatrice, her other young sister, chimed in. Of all her sisters, Beatrice was the most attached to their mother. She always followed her around and tried to emulate her every word and action.

"Thank you, Beatrice. I shall try to keep in mind how terrible horseback riding is for me," Thyra said, the sarcasm dripping from every word.

They filed out of the room. Thyra, dressed in a

crimson gown, ready for travel, was led by the women to the great hall. A large feast was already laid out, the tables laden with fruit and meat pies.

They would soon have to ride out to Gorm's ships. Her things had already been taken away up the stone road, down to the piers.

She squeezed Maud's hand for reassurance. This younger sister was the quietest of all the others, but she seemed to know when she was needed.

She was seated once more beside Gorm. He greeted her with a wink but restrained himself from anything that would raise eyebrows or set tongues wagging. Thyra was glad he wasn't insensitive. They may have teased each other, but this was different. It was a momentous day for her.

She was a bit unsure, now that the day had arrived.

It was over all too quickly. One by one, the brothers and sisters who were at hand bid her farewell. To her brother, the king, she knelt at his feet for his blessing. He gave it, raising her up and kissing both cheeks.

"Safe journey, sister."

She nodded and turned away from him to face her mother at last. Matilda was not a woman for tears. But Thyra, who had been in her company long enough by now, could tell she was grieving in her own way. Her smile did not reach her eyes, and her fingers kept reaching for her rosary beads. She doubted her mother ever loved anyone more than her father. She would go to her deathbed with his name still on her lips. The thought struck her then that she wouldn't be here to help lay her mother to rest. She would miss out on everything. From deaths to births, life would go on without her. She understood why it seemed that her mother could not look her in the eyes.

She was mourning her.

The minute she left her brother's halls, she would start to fade, becoming a dim memory until finally she would be forgotten. She glanced around at all the familiar faces. How long would it take for them to forget there was once a princess named Thyra who ran through these rooms?

Her heart clenched. Tears pricked at the corner of her eyes. Then she saw Gorm, dressed in his finery, his gaze expectant. She threw her arms around her mother's neck. The final tether to her old life.

"Be strong."

Those were the last words her mother said to her, and she took them to heart. She would be. With a nod, she pulled away and took Gorm's outstretched hand.

"Are you well?" he said, so low only she could hear.

"I will be," Thyra said. At the moment, she was sad for all she was leaving behind.

He led her up the gangplank to their ship. Men had already taken up their positions at the oars. There would be a long journey ahead until the wind would be strong enough to fill their sails.

"You are not alone. Stand tall," he said, his arms on her shoulders.

Thyra smiled and waved to the gathered people on

the dock. Her eyes on her family. Memorizing their faces.

He gave the command, in a language she did not understand, and the drummer took up his position.

The men below tightened their grips on the oars, and then, at another word from Gorm, they were off.

Thyra couldn't do it anymore. She turned away from all the faces she knew and looked to the horizon. Gorm led her to a seat and wrapped his heavy fur around her.

She was surprised to see him trade spots with another man, rolling up his sleeves and rowing along with everyone else. Was he not a king? No one else seemed to think this was peculiar. She would ask him later.

She gazed around the ship some more. Benches crossed the hull, connecting on the gangplank that ran down the center of the ship. Below the benches were packed goods and stores of food and fresh water to drink. There was little else on the ship besides a makeshift tent set up around the mast. She frowned. Where would they sleep? How would they cook their food?

She had not thought to ask Gorm about the specifics of their travels. When had there been time though? This had been such a fast arrangement. What felt like hours passed, and she kept looking over to Gorm, still rowing. She was beginning to feel utterly useless just sitting here watching and lonely with no one to talk to.

She tried to stand, but being unused to the rolling motion of the waves, she fell back into her seat. She was dazed and tried to get her bearings, suddenly overly aware of the rocking motion of the boat. Her stomach churned.

Then Gorm appeared before her.

"Are you all right? It's best you focus on the horizon."

She tried to smile but found it made her feel worse. "I just wanted to come talk to you. Or I... I don't know. I've been feeling useless," she said, her shoulders sagging.

"Well, first things first. You need to get your sea legs. Just practice standing, and if you feel sick to your stomach, just focus on the horizon. If that fails, run for the edge of the ship," Gorm said, a worried smile spreading across his face.

"Very well, Captain." she said, trying to look brave for him. This was the first time she wished she had brought a maid along with her. Gorm had brought a lady's maid for her, but she did not speak much English. Currently, she herself was down at the helm of the ship, seeking refuge from the wind. Thyra didn't mind it so much, but then again, she had Gorm's heavy furs.

At last, Thyra decided she would have to master her fear. She stood, her arm holding on to the mast. She stood clutching the mast for what seemed like forever, her eyes fixed on the horizon as Gorm had suggested. It worked at quieting the sickening feeling in her gut.

Finally, Thyra dared to take a step. If she let her legs go soft and simply move along with the ship's movement, she wasn't in danger of toppling over again.

With slow meticulous steps, she made it over to the other side of the boat.

Gorm had thrown her a smile as she walked past him.

She grinned back but had wobbled in that moment as she had stopped focusing.

The next awkward moment came when she had to relieve herself. She cursed herself for not having more knowledge.

She approached Ingrid with an embarrassed look on her face, and she guessed right away what was afoot. She showed her to the makeshift tent and set down a crude bucket for her.

She shrugged apologetically, but Thyra thanked her. She wouldn't have known what to do.

She still had not even asked Gorm where they would be sleeping tonight.

There were no fires, so their meal consisted of bread and salted fish. The bread was from her brother's own kitchens but would have to be eaten, as there was only so long that the loaves would last before becoming moldy.

Gorm urged her to eat more, but she shook her head. Her stomach still churned uncomfortably. She had always thought being at sea would be such a great adventure that, she hadn't taken time to consider the minute details such a venture would entail.

He stood stretching, readying to head back to the hull to row beside his comrades, but she stopped him with a hand on his lower arm.

"Where shall we sleep?"

He looked confused by her question. "On the boat."

"But where…I do not see a room to do so."

Gorm seemed to understand then what she was talking about. "We set up a big tent over the top of us.

From one end of the ship to another. A few of us stand watch while the rest sleep. We have blankets and furs so you shall not be cold. It's not as comfortable for you as a bed, perhaps, but it's better than sleeping on the ground, that's for sure."

Thyra nodded but felt uneasy at the prospect. She had been used to sleeping for so long with only her sisters for company. Now she would be sleeping among all these strange men and her husband. She looked at Gorm and hoped he would not try to be intimate with her tonight or any other night until they had privacy. She didn't know what things were like in Denmark but she wouldn't stand for this.

The wind had finally begun filling the sails of the three ships. The men seemed to drop where they sat, eager to rest their tired arms and backs.

Thyra helped Ingrid hand out rations to all the men. She didn't know what was expected of her, but she wanted to feel helpful. She didn't think she was too important to serve these weary men. Gorm seemed to approve of her jumping in without being asked.

After the men ate their fill, they called for ale and water, asking their kind queen to see that their thirst was satisfied. Some had a mischievous look on their face, and Thyra wondered what jests they were making behind her back.

Gorm was at her side as she filled a drinking horn or cup as it was handed to her, one after another, and handed it back to its owner.

"Fill their glasses halfway," Gorm said into her ear. "I don't need my men to get drunk."

"Very well," she said as she reached for yet another cup.

The burly man gave her a toothy grin, and she saw he was missing a few teeth. From the looks of him, he had lost them fighting, not from decay.

His smile died on his lips when he saw how little he received, but Thyra remained steady and pointed him to the water barrel if he wanted anything more to drink.

"That was Knud," Gorm said. "He's a good fighter, but don't let his appearance fool you. He's as gentle as a pup."

"What are you saying, Lord Gorm, to your wife? We cannot understand," Knud asked from the crowd. His tone was teasing, but Thyra spotted his dark mischievous eyes. He was up to something.

"I was begging my dearest wife to sing us a tune," Gorm said. She could not understand, but then he repeated what he said in English. He was quick with a falsehood. She wondered if he had ever lied to her.

The men seemed to agree. They stomped their feet and raised their glasses toward her.

"Would you honor us with a song?" Gorm asked. "I have not heard you sing before."

"And if we weren't trapped on a boat, you would never have heard me sing," Thyra said. "My voice is terrible. Please warn them of that."

"A lady with such a pretty face cannot have a bad voice." A man who understood English had heard her.

123

Laughter filled the boat. Gorm glared but seemed to take the compliment in a good-natured way.

"One song," Thyra said. "Then you shall have to make do without me."

They nodded and settled in to listen to her.

"I dreamed a dream last night
  of silk and fair furs,
  of a pillow so deep and soft,
  a peace with no disturbance..."

Thyra sang with all her might. The sea was windy, but she was glad that it hid most of her mistakes. She sang a song of the comforts of home, which seemed to have the approval of the men. Ingrid seemed to be familiar with the tune and joined her. Their two voices carried farther, and the drummer took up the beat.

At the end of the song, the men applauded and asked for another.

Thyra shook her head, but Ingrid seemed more than pleased to continue. The mischievous man from before jumped to his feet and helped her in the next song, wrapping his arm around Ingrid's shoulder in a way she thought was too familiar.

No one seemed to think anything was wrong with this.

Gorm held out his hand and she took it as he led her to a seat near the back of the boat.

"You sang well enough. I would not mind to hear you sing again," he said. "How are you feeling now?"

"Well enough," she said. "I have no appetite for food or drink."

"It's your first time out at sea. When I was a young lad, I remember throwing up for hours on my first voyage. At least the seas are calm for now."

"This is a calm sea?" Thyra said, listening to the waves hitting the side of the boat, the spray of seawater coming up over the edge.

"It is. Pray to your god we don't encounter anything fouler. We need all the luck we can get. It will take us a week to get to Denmark."

"It will?" Now Thyra was apprehensive. "I hadn't realized it would take us so long to get there."

"If all goes well," he added. "It will be all right. The time will pass by faster than you know it."

"What will I do all day? It's not like I can serve food all day."

He laughed. "Is that what you are worried about? I should have guessed with your productive spirit this would feel like a punishment to you."

Thyra watched him consider for a moment; then an idea sprang to mind.

"Well, if you are keen on helping, there is always mending to be done. The sails fray, the nets rip. You can help."

"I've never mended sails before," she said, though admitting her ignorance dented her pride. "But I'd be happy to try."

"It really isn't that hard. Just imagine it's any other

piece of cloth you have to tie together. Except the needle is bigger."

She nodded. "I'll ask Ingrid to show me." She looked over to the makeshift stage. She was still singing, the men applauding and striking up with songs of their own. What a brave, peculiar woman. She did not seem to mind so many eyes on her. That would be something Thyra would have to get used to. Back in England, she disappeared into the background.

6

To say she was happy to see land would have been an understatement.

She could jump for joy if her legs weren't so sore and stiff. She wasn't sure why they were stiff, from — either sitting too much or sleeping on the boat for God knows how many nights.

She wasn't sure if she would recommend this to any other newlyweds. It was impossible to get any privacy. Occasionally, they would steal kisses in the dead of night, the squeeze of a hand, a passing caress. That was all they could manage. Gorm was eager for more, but she had her dignity.

Besides, after a few more days at sea, even he had no longer been in the mood. His focus had been on making sure his small fleet of three ships made it safely into the harbor of his capital city. Their fresh food had run out, and they were left with preserved food, from dried figs to fish.

Thyra had felt the mood on the ship shift from being jovial to serious. Hardly anyone had smiled in the last day or so until they had recognized where they were.

For Thyra, this was all new, so she couldn't have known that they were getting close. She didn't know that the crag of rocks to the southwest meant they were a few days away from home until Gorm pointed them out to her.

"Are you ready, Princess?" he said, an arm around her waist pulling her close.

"I am," Thyra said simply. Then she took a step away from his embrace. "How shall it be? Shall we no longer be so informal together?"

"Little will change. This is not England. We don't stand too much for ceremony. You will see. But the people will want to greet you when we arrive. I hope you shall like your new home," Gorm said.

She looked at him, happy that he was so sincere in his concern for her.

"Well, first things first. Before I do anything else, I shall have to learn the language. I had been under the impression everyone spoke English. How foolish I was," she said, shaking her head.

"You will learn quickly. You already speak Latin, you know some Greek. What's Danish to all of that?"

She nudged him beneath his ribs. "Don't tease me."

They were approaching the harbor. The men took up their oars again, as the wind was dying down. By now Thyra could hear the bells ringing throughout the city off in the distance.

There were many ships docked in the harbor. More than she had ever seen before.

She looked at Gorm, who seemed unconcerned by this, so she didn't think much of it either.

They approached, and Thyra, making last-minute adjustments to her veil and dress, stood by Gorm's side, mimicking his proud stance. She would be a queen to these people. She would not cower. This was what she had wanted, wasn't it?

At last, the ship came to a stop.

"Careful stepping off," Gorm whispered to her.

She was glad for his warning, for to suddenly be on solid land was just as shocking as it had been to be on the rocking boat at sea. She would have to adjust and hope she did not throw up her breakfast.

There was a clamoring of people shouting for news and greetings being called.

Gorm stood in front of the gathering crowd, a wide smile on his face. His voice boomed over all the other voices.

First he spoke in Danish, then in English, and Thyra knew it was for her benefit.

"My good people, I bring you English goods in the hulls of ships and my bride, the English princess, Thyra. Please make her welcome and show her every respect, for she has won my heart," he said with a little bow toward her.

Thyra blushed deeply red but took his outstretched hand. Applause and cheers followed this, and she managed a smile.

They were escorted through the city, past several buildings made of stone and wood. She had never seen such peculiar roofs and designs before.

They arrived at a great long house in the center of the city. It was a dominating building. Out front, a peculiarly dressed man waited. His face was painted white with black markings over it. He wore a headdress of leaves, antlers, and twigs atop his head and long flowing robes.

She schooled her expression to be impassive. This man must be someone of great importance.

The man began chanting. Behind him another beat a small handheld drum.

Gorm knelt before him, and she knelt too.

"He is blessing us," Gorm said under his breath.

She nodded, keeping her gaze fixed on the ground. She wondered what the English priest would say when he saw this. Was he still here? Had the church been set up? She had never been a very religious woman, but now, after such a long journey, she desired to pray to God to thank Him for her safe deliverance.

At last, the man finished and Gorm helped her stand, her legs wobbly once more.

Now it was this holy man who bowed to them and stepped aside so they could walk through the entrance of the large building.

"Is this to be our home?"

Gorm nodded. "It will be, but it is not only our home. It is the heart of the community. You shall see most people congregate here in the evenings."

"I saw so many strange ships in the harbor. Are they all yours?"

"No," Gorm said, shaking his head. "We have many traders passing through here. Did you see those gates we passed through to get into the harbor? Many traders pay a pretty penny to rest safely within them. You shall see people from as far away as Russia."

She gaped at him. "I had not known."

"Surprised such heathens as ourselves can have such connections?"

Thyra frowned up at him. "I never called you heathens."

"Maybe you didn't, but I know what is said about us through Europe. It is all right. I am trying to change how the world sees us, but I also know it won't happen overnight."

"It's nicer to think you are in the right," She said. "And what of the Christian church that was to be built here?" she said.

"It is still standing. He's gained a small following, and the Christian traders that come through here are happy to stop to pray there."

"I am glad to hear that. With so many new things to learn, I'm glad I will have a piece of home with me."

They had arrived in the central room. A large open area with a huge firepit in the center. Above the high ceiling was cut a hole through which the smoke escaped out.

On a dais on the other side of the room was a raised chair, another set beside it.

"Ready?"

She nodded at him and he led her there.

"I am happy to be home!" Gorm said, turning to those gathered as he sat on his throne, "Tonight we shall celebrate and drink to our heart's content. Tomorrow I shall try to fix all of your problems."

Scattered laughter spread through the room.

Then the lords lined up, coming to pay their respects to Gorm, or at least that's what she thought they were doing, but no. It was her they were bowing to.

It was at her feet that they laid their gifts. Often they would say a few words and touch their armbands. She desperately wanted to know what was being said but didn't want to look like a fool for not knowing.

She hoped she appeared gracious enough, smiling at each and bowing her own head in thanks.

Gorm squeezed her hand reassuringly.

At last they seemed to be done. Gorm, seeing his men come in with chests, waved them over. They were opened to reveal treasure after treasure. These were doled out to each man who had paid her homage.

Thyra watched, entranced by the customs so unfamiliar to her. She was careful not to show any unease and just tried to soak it all in. She remembered how Gorm had hesitated over proposing to her all those years ago. He had known how hard it would be for a person to adapt to a new country.

The other striking thing she noticed was the number of women who left their hair uncovered. All of them had it braided or kept out of their face somehow, but rarely did she see a woman with a veil over her hair. At most she had seen them covered with little more than scarves. Thyra couldn't stop staring at the different hairstyles.

She felt out of place now with her own updo. Though for the moment there was nothing to see but a knotted mess of hair after over a week at sea.

The greeting quickly turned into a full-on celebration. Over the large firepit in the center of the room, they brought a recently slaughtered goat to roast. Other food was brought in as well, and everyone had their cup or tankard or drinking horn filled.

As the party kicked off, Gorm made his way to her side.

"You must be tired. Are you sure you would not wish to retire for the night?"

"With you?" she asked.

He shook his head. "I will have to stay. Hopefully, tomorrow I can find some time to rest."

"I would like to wash," Thyra said, whispering this request. "I feel like I am caked in brine, and soon I will become as dry as that fish of yours."

"Well, we can't have that," Gorm said with a sigh and looked around. He waved someone over. A woman in her thirties. Her plain clothes told Thyra that she was a servant, but she could be certain of little in this new land.

"Helga will take you to our rooms. I told her to help you bathe. I shall find Ingrid to keep you company and be your translator. Here's a quick lesson: *ya* means yes. *Nu* means no. *Du kan gå* means you are dismissed. Can you remember that?"

Thyra repeated everything back to him. The words felt weird on her tongue, but he smiled at her and kissed her full on the lips. "My clever princess."

"A Queen now, I believe," Thyra said with a haughty smile and a wink.

He laughed and patted her shoulders good-naturedly. "Yes. I shall try to remember."

Thyra followed the other woman, ready to get into clean clothes and sleep in a bed. The back of the long-house was divided into a few large rooms. Fewer than she would have thought, given the size of the place.

Helga opened one of the doors, motioning for her to follow her inside. The room was spacious. It was clearly used for more than just sleeping. There was a large desk off to one side as well as chests piled around the room. A small fireplace heated the room as well. She was sad there were no windows. Candles and the fireplace provided the only light. She wondered why that was.

The woman made a noise and seemed to be signing to her that she was to wait here. Thyra nodded and took a seat on a stool by the desk.

She could see rudimentary markings carved into the desk. Staring at it for a while, she realized it was a haphazardly drawn map. Was this Jutland?

There was only one book in the whole room, and it was in a language she didn't know, though it looked awfully similar to Latin.

She nearly dropped the book when a chorus of voices

sounded outside the room. Helga appeared with two other women carrying buckets of water.

A man followed behind with a large tub. He set it down in front of the fire and left the room without making eye contact with her.

Thyra watched as the women poured their buckets of water in. Steam rose from the tub. She wandered over to see. The water was still low, but the women indicated she could get in.

Thyra wasn't about to complain. It was better than a jug of water and a washcloth. They left the room, and only Helga stayed off to the back of the room.

Thyra was glad that she was left some degree of privacy.

She scrubbed her skin raw, and when the water had gotten too cold she finally got out of the tub. Dripping water on the floor until Helga rushed over with a towel and pointed to the clothes.

Thyra nodded her head in thanks. By this point, she felt very awkward about not being able to speak to her.

She had thrown her linen shift on when the door to the room opened again. She was glad to see Ingrid there. Her hair looked messier than usual, and she wore a slightly irritated expression.

She saw Thyra fiddling with her gown and said something scathing to Helga, who ran forward to help her dress.

"You shall have to learn our language quickly," Ingrid said, talking to her in English now. "Thralls will take advantage of you until you do."

"I don't mind. Helga was kind to me."

Ingrid shook her head. "You are the queen. Wife of Gorm. You must demand respect. No one gives it freely. Do you need any more food? Or anything else? Once you are dressed we will leave you."

"No, I am okay. I just want to rest. It's so dark in here..." She couldn't help but comment.

Ingrid looked at her, confused by her observation. "You need more candles?"

"No, I would have liked a window in the room."

"Window? But that would be so unsafe," Ingrid said, shaking her head. "You would freeze to death, or someone could climb in and slit your throat in the middle of the night."

Thyra's hand went to her throat subconsciously. "You are right, of course. I had not thought of that."

"England is very different," Ingrid said with an understanding look. "Anyway, do you need anything else, or shall I go?"

"No, I am fine. Thank you."

Thyra watched Ingrid leave without another word. Her curiosity to explore the room was overshadowed by her desire to sleep. So she was grateful that the room was so dark.

She blew out all the candles, but left the fire burning in the grate. She assumed it would be safe. It was small and it would provide her some light.

She sank onto the bed. Made uneasy by the stillness. After so long at sea, she had gotten used to the rocking motion. Her eyelids struggled to stay open, and she let herself drift off into the dark nothingness of her mind, still unable to believe where she was. There was so much to do, but that could wait for tomorrow.

A motion beside her jolted her out of sleep with a gasp.

"Hush, go back to sleep. I didn't mean to disturb you, Thyra," Gorm's now familiar voice said in the dark.

Her heart still pounded in her chest, but she nodded and sank back down into her pillow. She listened to Gorm groan as he stretched out on the bed.

"Good night," he said with a yawn.

"You too." Thyra could already feel herself falling asleep.

———

HER FIRST OFFICIAL day as queen of Denmark felt unremarkable. More than anything, she felt like a child again. Unsure of how to behave and what to say or do. Gorm had let her sleep in, but she had awoken in the dark with only a few dying embers in the fireplace for light.

She had cracked open the door to let in the light and found Helga sitting down outside her room.

The woman nodded to her and stepped in. Thyra had not been given much time to get her bearings. Helga helped her dress, and Thyra asked her to braid her hair. She had decided she would simply wear her veil and circlet today and not the full head covering she had arrived in.

Then she wondered what to do. She couldn't twiddle her thumbs in this room forever. Helga was no help; it wasn't only the fact they couldn't speak, but she was a servant and wasn't about to make suggestions to her.

Finally, she decided to go find her husband. "Gorm?"

Helga seemed to understand and led the way out to the main hall.

It seemed to be late in the morning; the hall had been cleaned out and the sun was high in the sky already.

Gorm was not sitting on his throne, but Helga, after asking one of the passing men a question, led her outside.

It was then that Thyra noticed the change in climate. Yesterday, with all her nerves, she had not felt the chill in the air. It was nearly September, but still this felt colder than what she was used to.

She followed in step with Helga to what looked like a workshop built near the main building. The sound of metal being hammered rang through the air.

Helga pointed for her to go in, but she remained outside with her head bowed.

Throwing her shoulders back, Thyra stepped inside. It was the blast of heat that first surprised her, then the smell of burning metal that assaulted her senses.

"Thyra! Glad to see you on your feet," Gorm said as he noticed her.

"Good morning, Lord Gorm," she said with a respectful curtsy to him.

He seemed amused by her show of respect. A man was working over an anvil with a hammer in his hand. He barely glanced up, he was so focused on his work.

"This is Olaf. He is the best weaponsmith in all of Denmark and one of my most trusted commanders," Gorm said, noticing her glance toward him. "He also doesn't enjoy being interrupted. You needed something?"

She nearly laughed. Of course she needed something. She needed everything. She felt so lost. But Thyra kept control over herself.

"Shall we talk outside then, milord?"

Gorm nodded. "But no need to be so formal." And he kissed her on the mouth.

Thyra, not in the mood, pushed him away with a frown. He looked apologetic but also amused.

Once outside, she rounded on him. "Gorm, what am I supposed to do? I assume you haven't brought me here to just sit in that dark room waiting for you to use me as some bed slave." Thyra hadn't meant to sound so crude, but really she couldn't help her growing temper. This was his home and he slipped right back into everyday life, but it was not hers.

"That would not be an unappealing prospect," he said, giving her a heated look that told her he desired her. She fought the warm feeling growing in her belly, pushing it down. This could not stand. Seeing she would not budge, he relented. "You are right. I got pulled away by my duties very quickly. I promised I would help you adjust, but I have not kept my word. I have not forgotten though. What would you like to do?"

Thyra bit her lip, considering. Above all else she wanted to be useful, but...

"I want to learn to speak your language. I feel dumber than a child having to mime what I want. Poor Helga must think I'm a simpleton."

"Don't worry about some thrall. But if that is what you want first, then I shall command our best of teachers to come teach you every day until you are fluent in Danish. Anything else?"

She raised her hands in a gesture that said there was so much more she wanted but couldn't quite say. "I don't know. I have no idea what is expected of me. Please tell me. Show me."

"Learn our language, be at my side. I'm sure you can find plenty of busywork to do, but there are many people that can darn socks and fix my clothes. What I would really want is someone that I could trust while I am away. So focus on learning. Then we will see. And if you occasionally invite me to your bed, I promise I won't object."

He said the last part in such seriousness it took a moment for his words to sink in. She swatted at his arm and then wondered if that was not acceptable to do to a King. As he laughed, Thyra took him in. His shirt and pants were all well-made and of good quality, but they would not look out of place on any worker. He did not look like a King at all. She thought of her brother in his long robes, the crown on his head, his self-importance.

"I shall come find you in a few hours. Have you eaten yet?"

She shook her head. No.

"Very well, stay in the hall. I'm sure there are many

who will come keep you company. Eat something and I'll see about getting you started with some tutors."

"Can I go to see the church?"

"Oh, yes. I forgot. I'll escort you there myself tonight."

"Usually we pray in the morning."

"Tomorrow then," he said with a shrug.

Thyra frowned. What sort of church was being run here anyway? She watched as Gorm had a few words with Helga. She was glad there was to be some sort of plan for her. What if she hadn't spoken out? Would she still be waiting in that dark room?

There were so many questions she still had, but Gorm was right. One thing at a time. She would figure things out eventually. Again, she remembered how he worried that his bride would have a tough time with a new country. She would prove to him that he had not made a mistake, that she could adapt. This was certainly more adventure than she could have ever dreamed of.

In the end, she spent the day among the other women, eating with them, watching them tend to their chores and children. She couldn't participate in their conversation yet. Ingrid was nowhere to be found and none of them spoke English. They smiled at her occasionally and offered for her to hold a baby.

Gorm had come in as promised with a man in tow, named Olev. He would teach her Danish and all the important rituals. She did not recognize him, but Gorm informed her later that this was the head priest who had blessed their union. He had taken it upon himself to teach her their ways.

"He wants you to become a good pagan wife to me and not convert me to Christianity," Gorm whispered in her ear at dinner, when she asked why the high priest would take such an interest in her.

She shot him a quizzical look. "You can't be serious."

"Oh, I'm deadly serious. So if you want to keep my people's good opinion, don't go converting everyone you see. I am not asking you to pray to the old gods, but don't meddle with my people's beliefs either." This he said in a more serious tone.

"I wouldn't dream of it."

"Your brother hopes for it. The Pope thinks you might be the gateway to more missionaries," Gorm said.

"And yet you still married me?" Thyra said, puzzling over what he told her. She had not known too much about this. She had no desire to convert anyone.

"I figured you did not seem so zealous. You seemed agreeable and interested in my gods. You must understand we have many gods. Your Christian god is no threat. He can join the rest if He wishes. But like I said, I will not force people to worship Him."

"I understand. I agree with you. What about me? I don't know your gods. Will I be asked to worship them?" she said, not adding that she would refuse to convert, even for her husband. The Bible taught her that she should cleave to him, but it had not specified what to do in the case of a pagan husband.

He shook his head. "It is more complicated than that.

You have already shown them respect by wearing my armband, by listening to the high priest's blessing. They demand nothing more, as long as you don't try to undermine them. Other than that, nothing else is required. However, as my queen, I will expect you by my side for festivals."

"I suppose that is reasonable. A show of outward unity."

"Everything is always so methodical with you. You would make a good commander."

Thyra smiled, enjoying the preposterous image of her leading an army into battle.

"After you go to see your church, there is someone I would like you to meet. She lives outside the city walls, but it is not a long journey. Do you feel up for it?"

"Who is this woman?"

He looked like he was debating with himself about whether or not he would keep her guessing. She nudged him under the table with her foot, letting him know she was not in the mood for games.

"She is a wise woman, very old. She also happens to be my grandmother."

Thyra gasped. "She's still alive? She must be old indeed."

Gorm nodded. "She has been blessed by the gods. She is over sixty years old. As she will tell you herself, she has lost count and is living with one foot in the other world."

"Why does she not live here?"

"The work she does is important. The noise of the

town drowns out the voices of the gods. She will visit occasionally, especially when I force her if I fear an attack."

Thyra nodded, still confused about how everything worked. Why had she always seen the world as though every country operated like England? Her own ignorance made her feel inferior and self-conscious. Gorm, who was so well traveled, had been able to acclimatize himself much better to life in England. She wondered how he did it. Through practice, most likely.

When they had first met, he must have been just above ten years old himself. By contrast, she had never been outside the insular world of the English court.

"I would be honored to meet her. I am intrigued. Do you have any other family members? I can't believe I didn't think to ask before now."

Gorm shook his head. "None living now. My mother died giving birth to my sister, who did not long survive her. My father in battle. If I have any half brothers or sisters, I am not aware."

"I am sorry," Thyra said. Her hand enveloped his. "You must have been lonely."

"I was hardly allowed to feel lonely," Gorm said, though he appeared graver. "I am glad to finally have settled down with a wife and start a proper family."

"Do you expect me to provide you with a very large dynasty, then? Because I don't remember discussing that," she said, grinning.

"Then you should learn to bargain better." He leaned over, kissing her. This was not some light peck on the lips, and she turned away from him. It was not his attention that she did not enjoy, but she hated feeling as though everyone's eyes were on her.

"It may be acceptable in Denmark to act like this, but it is not in England," she said in response to his questioning gaze.

"Well, as long as you are not mad at me," he said in a lighthearted tone, but she could see he was not pleased.

How could she explain to him that this sort of behavior would have her labeled as some common whore? She could imagine her mother hearing about it, even from this far away. It would take more than an ocean to keep her reprimands from reaching her. Thyra wouldn't be surprised if she flew across the ocean propelled by her anger alone.

She squeezed his hand. "I am adjusting still. I was raised learning that such public displays of affections were wanton and sinful."

Gorm shook his head. "I'll never understand this custom. I am glad I have rescued you away from it."

There was a twinkle of mirth in his eyes.

Thyra replied in kind. Last night, she had read to him from the tales of King Arthur. Tales she had written on paper herself. Lots of great ladies were rescued from towers in those days, it seemed.

As GORM PROMISED, they took a small retinue to go to the church. They did not ride their horses through the sometimes narrow streets, but led them by their reins.

The building was on a small outcrop among many buildings. She would never have noticed it except for the large cross on top. It was made of gilded metal and seemed to catch the light. Such a gaudy piece did not suit the building well and looked pretentious rather than pious.

At the sound of their arrival, the priest stepped out in his dark brown robes. A simple belt of braided rope around his waist and a wooden cross hanging from his neck.

He bowed when he saw them, his eyes resting upon hers longer than anyone else.

"It is a pleasure to meet you, Father John," Thyra said with a small curtsy, seeing that no one in her party had the inclination to speak. "I wished to come see your church and pray in the chapel. Are you well?"

"I am very well," he said, though his eyes couldn't quite meet hers.

"Well, let us go inside," she said, handing off the reins to Gorm.

He showed no inclination to go inside with her.

Like all Danish houses, there was very little light that came in. Candles were burning before the altar. The center of the room had the same sort of long hearth she had seen in her own great hall.

"Some adjustments were made, my lady. I had arrived with a small stained-glass window, but after the first winter here, I gave up any hopes of having it installed," Father John said, gesturing to the small pane of glass now propped up behind the dais.

"It's still beautiful," Thyra said, looking around at the pews. They were roughly put together. Planks of wood with crude legs attached at the bottom. She thought she even spotted a barrel. The crucifix was the focal point of the room. It, at least, was not put together shoddily. "Have you met with much resistance?"

Father John gave a light shrug. "I was provided with the necessary funds by your brother. Lord Gorm was kind enough to supply what was lacking. There were costs I did not consider when I set out on this mission. But I am glad you are here, my lady. Perhaps we shall have our own congregation and outfit the church properly. Maybe even move to more suitable accommodations."

She frowned, looking around. Though the house was small it would seem sufficient, given she was likely going to be the only regular visitor.

"How many come here to pray?"

"We get the odd trader here and there. Most of the locals are not interested in the word of God but just come in to ogle at the sacred ceremony of the Mass. There are thralls that come in, but they have no funds to donate. I have tried to speak to Lord Gorm about this, but he seems unable to control his people. Or unwilling."

It was hard not to notice the slight scathing tone with which he spoke.

"I shall see what I can do, but you should be encouraging the locals to show interest. How else will they open their hearts to the Bible and the Christian faith?"

He didn't like being corrected by her. He seemed to take on a stony countenance. "Of course, my lady. You are correct." He bowed.

She prayed before the altar, trying to clear her head of his complaints. She smelled the familiar scent of burning incense, and a feeling of homesickness overcame her. She had to fight back the tears as she thought of her home.

Nothing was going to be easy, was it? But what would have been the fun in that?

When she got up, she crossed herself before the altar and handed the priest a gold coin—not that he deserved it, she thought.

He was happy enough to take it.

Despite his complaints, he seemed to be well fed. There should be no reason why he was so despondent, but she could understand how isolating it was to be in this new place. At least she had a husband.

They had started a game of bones outside. Gorm was happy to see her reappear.

"I was worried I'd have to come rescue you," he said. "Have you finished?"

She nodded. "Thank you for letting me come."

The men packed up their belongings, and they began their walk to the main street that passed through the city. Once there, they mounted their horses and set off at a fast pace toward Gorm's grandmother's.

It was a beautiful landscape. Lots of tall hills and mountains. Her horse was stocky and strong. He was not as tall as her old horse, but she could feel how surefooted he was on the rocky terrain. Her own horse back in England would have been unused to the landscape. It was beneficial to ride on smaller horses on this sort of road. In fact, there wasn't much of a road at all, just a well-beaten trail.

They rode until midday. As they approached the first crop of trees, they dismounted and walked.

Thyra was taken aback by the entranceway.

On two sticks on either side of the gate were perched skulls of some unknown animal. Feathers and beads stuck to them.

She looked to Gorm, but his eyes were focused on the trail ahead.

Only the pair of them proceeded through the gate, with Gorm carrying a heavy fur in one hand.

"Watch your step," he said, holding on to her hand with his free hand.

The path was bumpy, and the rocks on the path seemed to act more as a deterrent to any visitor than a help.

They walked through a small field of vegetables and herbs. A small building she could only describe as a hut became visible. Hidden by the growth of heavy vines and bushes.

It was then Thyra noticed the small woman standing in the doorway. She had imagined an old, bent over woman but this woman was standing tall. Dressed in a dark gown and a headdress similar to the one she had seen on the high priest.

At her side, Gorm bowed low once they were a few steps away from the doorway.

Thyra met the woman's intense gaze and bowed as well.

"Come in."

Her voice was deep and seemed to echo around them. Thyra noted that they were at the foot of a mountain, hills on all three sides acting as natural protection for her and the reason behind the echo she heard.

Still, she followed behind Gorm with a sense of awe.

His grandmother seated herself on a great chair at the other end of the hearth. A large fire burned brightly.

"Be seated," she said, motioning to the two chairs set out on the side opposite of her.

In silence, Gorm complied and Thyra, not wanting to upset anyone, complied as well.

She nearly jumped out of her chair when the wise woman began chanting. The sound carried through the hut, enveloping them and silencing the outside world. She threw something in the fire and their senses were overwhelmed by something potent. Thyra could see a variety of jars on the shelves, the skin of a snake tacked up on one wall. Bones of various shapes and sizes in a basket. She shivered. She had never seen a witch, but this is what she imagined they looked like.

"Oh, gods, bless this marriage. This union between two people of two nations. May their countries be united as they have been. May their marriage be fruitful and carry on their alliance."

Thyra was shocked by the English words.

Gorm smiled down at her and she knew the grandmother was doing this for her benefit.

Her chant turned away from English and returned to a language she did not understand. More powders were thrown into the fire.

She thought she smelled pepper and cloves. Maybe some thyme.

Thyra felt as though the room was beginning to spin. She could see the whites of the woman's eyes. What was happening?

"Pass me the bag, child."

"She means you." Gorm nodded.

Thyra looked down and saw a bag in front of her. She had not noticed it when she first sat down.

Tentatively, but without hesitation, she approached the woman and handed her the bag as instructed.

"You do not waver. This is good."

Thyra, not sure if she should go sit back down, waited by her side as the chanting continued. Then she threw the bag upside down into the ring of bones in front of her. A variety of things came pouring out, arranging themselves as they fell in some pattern that only the woman seemed to understand.

The wise woman pondered the bones, the feather, the stones. Then looked up at her.

Thyra saw how weathered her face was. She had

never seen such an old person before. She had almost an unworldly appearance.

She nodded over the bones, then regarded her with a smile, and Thyra saw the woman had maybe one or two teeth left to her.

"Your fate has been tied to this country since your birth. You are strong and that is good, for you will need it. The gods smile on this marriage. You need not fear their disapproval." She spoke in broken English. Then she turned to Gorm and seemed to repeat what she'd said, but with much more detail.

"You may tell her later. The words don't come to me as easily as they used to."

Thyra was dying to ask her how she knew English, but for now she was in awe of this woman and dared not speak in case she insulted her or interrupted some great ritual.

She returned to her seat and watched as the matriarch swept everything back into the bag. She reached into another pouch at her side and sprinkled something into the fire.

"Salt for cleansing. The ritual is done. I welcome you. I welcome you both," she said, her arms falling back to her sides.

Now that the fire had died down and Gorm helped her remove her ritual garment, his grandmother seemed to transform from a powerful sorceress into the small figure of a woman.

"Make me some porridge, will you," she said out loud.

Thyra stood, expecting that it was to her she was speaking, but it was Gorm who busied himself around the kitchen without another word. He knew where everything was and seemed practiced at this.

She had everything she could need at hand. A water barrel in the corner beside her pots and pans. Dried goods tucked away on shelves away from the rodents that might try to pilfer a few morsels.

It was a cozy home. Thyra was still reeling from everything she had witnessed.

"Come closer, child. My eyes aren't what they used to be."

Her words broke her out of her thinking.

Thyra did as she was asked.

"What may I call you, lady?"

"My name is Olga. Now, you may wish to ask how I came to know your tongue. Well, my mother was English too."

"Really?" Thyra was intrigued. "I had not known there was another royal marriage back then between our nations, but I know little of our own history."

Olga chuckled, a low raspy sound. "Not so much a marriage. Back in those days, us Norsemen raided your shores. Your brother would not have wanted it known, but at one point we conquered more than half your lands. My mother was a thrall, but my father fell in love with her and married her."

"Thrall? Is that what you call English people?"

Thyra's question elicited a snort of laughter from Gorm stirring the pot of porridge over the hot embers.

"Thrall is a slave," he said by way of explanation. "They are like your servants."

Thyra frowned. "I did not know English people were taken as slaves."

"It is the fate of those who aren't as strong or well defended as others. It is the way of the world."

Thyra wanted to disagree, but now was not the time or the place. He was right: it seemed to be a way of life for them. Who was she to start quoting to him from the Bible about how this was morally wrong? She could see how he would quote back to her how a woman's obedience is to her husband and he wouldn't even be wrong.

She shelved that topic for now.

His grandmother seemed able to read her thoughts and laughed.

"You will cause great chaos with your coming. But it will be for the good of all. You are right not to rush."

Thyra looked down at her hands in her lap. She hadn't meant to be such an open book about her feelings.

Gorm served them piping hot porridge, which he sweetened with honeyed dates. For himself, he pulled out dried meat that he chewed on while frowning at the pair of them.

Thyra ignored his distemper and instead proceeded to speak to his grandmother as best she could, as her English, while good was still hard to understand sometimes. It had mixed in with the local dialect.

"Come back to me next summer after you have learned some more of my native tongue. It will be easier to speak then," Olga said, patting her knees.

The pat was heavy and Thyra got the impression that Olga, despite her age and appearance, was stronger than she looked.

"I have something before you go," she said and moved over to the kitchen. She was examining the shelves and pulled down a few jars. Gorm came to sit by her side, and they both watched her at work, humming an old tune.

"You are not mad at me, are you?" he asked under his breath.

Thyra shook her head. "What sort of wife would I be if I argued with my husband in the first month of marriage?"

He grinned. "A pretty typical one, I'd say."

"Well, I am always trying to surprise you," she said with the hint of a smile on her lips. "Besides, this is a matter greater than myself. I will not fight a battle I am going to lose."

His eyebrow rose.

She leaned toward him. "I shall wait for my chance to strike. So I can make sure I win every argument."

Before he could reply, she planted a firm, challenging kiss on his lips.

"I don't think you will need this," came the laughing sound from Olga.

Thyra looked up and saw Olga walking over to them with a small pouch.

"Add this to a cup of boiling water and drink it every night."

"Why?"

"Venerable grandmother, are you trying to give her

fertility drafts?" Gorm said, looking at the pouch with skepticism.

Thyra nearly dropped the pouch. Children? Now? She wasn't sure.

"When it is time. Who knows, maybe she is already with child, but this does more than improve fertility. It gives a woman strength and energy. She will need ample amounts of that."

Gorm exchanged a few words with her that Thyra couldn't understand. But her mind was wandering now. There had been so much to learn and see that she had not even thought of the genuine possibility of children.

Noticing the silence that fell about the room, Thyra looked up. Olga was considering her.

"Dear child. There is no need to fear. Women love these sorts of charms and potions. But I may have something else you would like just the same." She went back to her workbench and picked up a premade pouch. She sniffed the contents inside and nodded.

"Here. If you are not ready for children, then take this every night without fail. Wait until your courses have come before you take them. If you are already carrying a child, taking this would spell disaster for you and the babe you carry."

Thyra ignored Gorm's grunt of disapproval and took the offered pouch. This was sinful magic, but the thought of putting off having children was all too tempting.

Gorm took their dishes out to clean them in the stream that ran by his grandmother's garden. Thyra helped her unpack the supplies he had brought her.

Wrapped in the fur were dried fish and meat, and a cooked pie from the night before.

"Gorm is a good man," Olga told her. "I can see the two of you will work well together. In times of struggle, turn to each other, and though you are not ready now, perhaps before I am called away by the gods you will present me with my first great-grandchild."

Thyra smiled. "I shall promise to do so. Do you think Gorm is upset?"

Olga laughed. "What business is it of men what we decide to do? We rule our bodies, not them. If he tries to tell you any different, you send him my way and I'll put him right."

She had to chuckle alongside her.

"That sounds good."

"Take care, Thyra. Visit me often before the snows come."

"Will you not spend winter at Jelling with us?" Thyra asked, looking around. It must be very dull living here by yourself.

Olga shook her head. "I am surrounded by ghosts here. I do my work in peace and tranquility. Gorm makes sure I don't freeze to death. Don't you, Gorm?"

Thyra turned her head and saw Gorm had reentered the house in a better mood.

"I might change my mind, but yes, I will still come look after you."

"Good boy."

"I am a king now, Grandmother. You should remember to address me as one."

Gorm was puffing out his chest importantly, but Thyra could see by his manner that he was joking.

Olga's response was quick. As he walked by her to deposit the bowls on the table, she yanked him down by the ear. Thyra didn't think she could move that fast.

"Listen here, boy, I have lived three times more than you have and will live longer than you. I owe you no respect, son of my son."

"I am sorry."

At his words, she released him suddenly, and he staggered back.

Thyra watched the exchange with amusement pasted on her face.

Now that their business was concluded, Gorm escorted her back to the horses. On the walk back, he asked her not to speak of what she had heard or seen.

"Especially not the reprimand?" Thyra asked with a smile.

"Especially not that," Gorm said, rubbing his left ear. His grandmother's grip had been unrelenting.

To extend their honeymoon, Gorm had took her on a short excursion to a trading port south of Jelling. They spent a week on the road, sleeping under tents. Thyra was enjoying taking in the new sights but was also glad to have a proper meal in the city. Unlike Jelling, Haithabu was not as prosperous. She could see it in the faces of those who lived there. The people, from the youngest to the oldest were noticeably gaunt and looked exhausted.

Gorm explained that they were under constant risk of raiding from the Germans. Every spring they would plant their fields, and by summer they would be destroyed by the incursions. They had to rely on the sea for their food. The money they made from trade sustained them but it was not a pleasant sort of life.

"One day I wish to fortify this town. I know it has the potential to be a great trading post."

Gorm took her to the wall his people called Danevirke. It was not far from the city. Much like Hadrian's Wall much of it had fallen into ruin.

"This is where we hold the line with the Germans," he showed her as they walked along the moss-covered wall. "Once this wall had stopped their incursions but now it has become a relic of the past."

"Why not rebuild?" Thyra placed a hand on the cold stone.

"We hardly have the time and resources. The Germans keep encroaching on our lands. It takes all our efforts to push them back. I am stretched too thin to take on another project that might end in failure."

She nodded feeling she could not press him further. She didn't know this kingdom. At least not yet.

***

LIFE IN JELLING was challenging at first. Once they returned from their travels it took Thyra a few weeks to get the hang of where everything was in the city. They did not move around like they had in England, but people were always coming and going.

In the market square, farmers came to sell their wares, but unlike in England, these were no ordinary farmers. They were warriors, ready to pick up an axe when the need arose. More often than not, they went raiding in the summer months, leaving the farm to be taken care of by their wives or thralls.

She had not discussed with Gorm the powders his grandmother had given her. Thyra now wished that she had done so in private. He had said nothing to her, which she took to mean that he would respect her wishes, but... she could also tell he was not pleased.

One day, as they were lying side by side in their grand bed, the darkness hiding her from his scrutiny, she brought it up as gently as she could.

"Gorm, husband? Are you awake?"

She heard his grunt by way of reply.

"I want children. I wanted to tell you that. What I don't want is to have a child when I am all alone here, unable to speak to anyone except a few people. Can you understand that?"

Silence.

Thyra sighed, fighting back her own irritation. She wanted to be calm and collected. "I am alone here. I have so much to learn. Can you give me some time?"

"And the two years?"

She took a deep breath. "I know. I wasn't thinking. Or perhaps I didn't want to face the very real implication of what coming here would be like. I do not regret my choice, but I need some time to adjust. I know you need an heir, and I too would like to have children. One day."

She heard him shuffle, then turn around away from her. Thyra assumed the conversation was done. She went over in her mind what had been said. She had to accept that he would be upset. No man wanted a wife who was unwilling to give him children. Still, she refused to relent. Her feelings were valid too. She could just imagine the hilarity of going into labor with a midwife who she could not communicate with. She was sure it had been done before, but she wasn't about to volunteer herself. As brave as she was, Thyra was frightened by the mere thought of childbirth, let alone giving birth alone. Her mother had been incredibly lucky or blessed by God to have gone through the ordeal so many times and come out alive.

Many women she had known were buried within a year of their marriage. Still, this was their lot in life, dating back to Eve and Adam.

She couldn't dwell on the negatives, for she had seen what depression could do to a person too.

The next few days, she went steadily about her business. She sat with her tutors, worked with the women, and ate by Gorm's side. As often as she could, she would walk to the church to pray.

Lately, she had begun praying for patience.

Then one morning, out of nowhere Gorm appeared in the hall, earlier than he usually did. Behind him followed a woman Thyra had not yet met. She seemed to be arguing with him about something but stopped short when she spotted Thyra.

Gorm bowed to Thyra, placing a courtly kiss on her hand as he had seen was the custom in England.

"I hope you are having a good morning, my lady. I wish to present someone to you." Still holding her hand, he helped her to her feet and walked her over to the strange woman.

"This is Ursa, the greatest shield-maiden to ever walk these shores."

The woman bowed from the hip. It was then Thyra noticed that she was dressed in pants, but that wasn't the most peculiar thing about her. That prize had to go to the axe hanging from her belt.

"A pleasure to meet you too, Lady Ursa," Thyra said, looking from the stranger to Gorm.

"I'm no lady, and don't try to butter me up with flattery, King Gorm. I won't do it."

"Do what?" Thyra was curious, though she was getting a sneaking suspicion she knew what this was about.

"When we were engaged, I promised you a tutor in the art of war... and here she is." His hands moved in a flourish, as if he was presenting her with Ursa again.

"I would have thought this teacher would have been willing..."

"Wife, you demand so much of me. Besides, Ursa will do it. Won't you?"

At times like these, Gorm's playfulness shone

through. He was a troublemaker. Mischievous as the trickster Loki.

Thyra looked apologetically at Ursa, who was busy sizing her up as well.

"Is it true you wanted to learn to fight?"

Thyra blinked. This entire conversation felt more like a dream or a nightmare than reality, and it took a moment for her words to sink in.

"I did express a wish to learn," she said, hearing how hesitant she was. Wasn't this one of the very things she had dreamed of as a child? She had brushed it aside, believing that it was an impossible dream.

Ursa regarded her for a moment. "If you are serious, I will teach you, but I will not go easy on you just because you are the wife of Lord Gorm. Do you understand?"

"Oh, yes, of course." Thyra sounded more like a child than the dignified Queen she wished to appear as.

"I'll see you at dawn. On the beach. You should wear something suitable for moving in."

Thyra looked down at her long dress and gulped. She wasn't sure how she felt about pants, but she nodded. If she was about to learn how to wield weapons, her wearing pants would be the least of her concerns. Besides, the rules were different here. She needed to embrace them.

Ursa gave her another nod and a bow and left. Her cape swirling around her at her abrupt exit.

"She's not too pleased with me," Gorm said after she was out of sight. "But I am glad she will teach you. She had been very resistant to accept the task. She must have seen something about you that she liked."

"What could she have seen?"

"Well, it helped that you could meet her eyes. Most people are terrified of her. You also had a twinge of hero worship in your eyes. I can't pretend I am not jealous. Maybe one day you will regard me with such reverence," Gorm said, trying his best to look piteously at her.

"Why would people be terrified?" Thyra said, ignoring him.

"Well... you will see. One way or another. Are you happy?"

"Of course I am." Thyra placed a hand over her heart. "I don't think I can believe it, to be honest."

He gave her a quick peck on the lips. "I am sorry for being upset. I hope that we can work together in the future—side by side. It always helps to have a happy wife at home, while I go off raiding."

Thyra chuckled. "Well, I am glad we can move past this so easily. I really am grateful, and I am sorry that I am not ready yet. Thank you for understanding."

He nodded, looking more solemn now than before. "I never had a proper family, but I hope to have one with you. I should warn you that soon I will have to leave to patrol my borders and settle disputes in other provinces. I will not be at your side for much longer. Once winter sets in, I will return. Take advantage of me while you have me here."

"When are you to leave?"

"Within the next week or two." He held her hand, seeing her frown deepen. "Don't worry."

"I can still barely speak to anyone..."

"You'll be surprised how fast you learn under pressure. I am sorry, but I was away from my duties for far too long."

Thyra nodded. What he said was true. She couldn't fault him. In fact, she was more than grateful he had stayed in the first place.

THE HEAVY CAPE around her was wrapped tight. Thyra felt strange in the leggings Gorm had given her. She wore a tunic that went down to her knees, feeling that anything shorter would make her too uncomfortable.

She was escorted down to the beach by a curious Ingrid and found Ursa waiting. They weren't alone on the beach. There were a lot of other women around too. Many were stretching. Others were dueling each other or going through their exercises.

Thyra took in the shields, axes, and even a sword or two. This seemed so out of place and foreign to her, but she was glad she would not be alone with Ursa. Though now that she thought about it, perhaps that would be better than embarrassing herself in front of all the other women.

"Lady," Ursa said with that curt bow of hers.

"Am I late?" Thyra looked around to everyone else.

Judging by how sweaty some of them looked, they had been practicing for quite some time.

"Not at all. Some come to train even earlier because they have business elsewhere. Let's walk." Ursa took her up and down the beach. The sand made it hard for Thyra to keep up. After a while, every step felt like a struggle. She had always thought of herself as an active sort of person. She was surprised to find that she was quickly getting out of breath. It was making it difficult to listen to what Ursa was saying. She had started talking to her about something called Valkyries.

Ursa finally noticed that Thyra had fallen behind. She smiled at her. The sort of smile one gave to a child when they tried to do something beyond themselves.

"First, we shall have to work on your strength and endurance. One reason we come to train on the beach is that it helps soften the blow when we fall. But another is that it helps increase the strength in our legs. It is much harder to walk or even run on sand than it is on dry land. Every day, you should come walk for a good hour or so."

"And when will I learn to wield weapons?" Thyra couldn't help asking, despite knowing she would sound like a petulant child.

"First you will become stronger. It would do us no good to show you how to lift a sword or throw an axe if you will be out of breath within five minutes." Ursa understood. In fact, she seemed to approve of Thyra's eagerness. "I have not met many foreign women so interested in learning."

"I admit I am rather an oddity, but I grew up chasing

after my brothers, not playing with my sisters. I was always envious of them."

"Battle is serious. Defending one's home is a precious skill to possess. Knowing how to fight for your life is too. In this life, we must fight for every day we live." Ursa went on. "Men always act as though women don't perish in battle. If the world was so simple, then I would not have bothered learning how to fight myself. I would have been content to sit by the fire until old age took me."

Thyra smiled. "That would be a nightmare. I have been sequestered by a fire long enough to know how boring that can be. More draining than this." She waved a hand over the beach.

Ursa shrugged. "I'll ask you in a year what you would prefer. Do you see that woman over there? Her name is Ygril. She speaks a bit of English too. If I am not around, she will help you. I have instructed her. Come every day around this time, or earlier if you dare. Get used to wearing those pants. Fighting in a dress is like fighting with your arms tied behind your back. Good luck."

"What shall I do now?"

"Walk. Up and down the beach. Until your legs start shaking and you collapse."

Thyra steeled herself. If this was what it took, then very well.

IT FELT as though every night Thyra was collapsing into bed and was asleep before she could even pull the blanket over herself. Between training in the morning and learning her husband's language, which she still struggled to pronounce, she was exhausted. Slowly, she learned that she should be arranging the food every night for dinner, checking the stores, brewing ale. Ingrid showed her to the market where she could buy things like honey to sweeten the ale. There was also this honey cake that Gorm seemed to love that she tried to make for him every night.

Gorm was now gone for weeks at a time. There were constant skirmishes at the border with the Germans. Farmers there had asked for his help, as they were constantly being raided.

She felt uneasy every time he left. He had promised her he would not fall in battle, but that was the promise of a man to a woman. How could he know what the future held?

Often Thyra found herself mulling over what future she would have here if something were to happen to Gorm. What would become of her? Would she return home to England?

One day, new ships were spotted in the harbor. The captain said he had a message for the queen of Denmark, Thyra.

She had been curious to see who it was from. She assumed it was from her family, for who else would be writing to her? In fact, most people did not even refer to her as a queen here.

"Your Grace, this is a letter from your brother, the king." The captain had come himself, bowing. Thyra saw how his eyes traveled around the longhouse, taking in the strangeness of everything as she had once done.

With great interest, Thyra broke the seal on the letter. She was taken aback by the writing inside. It was not Athelstan's smooth clear handwriting she was looking at but Edgar's. She could tell from the way he curled his *a*'s, a terrible habit from the schoolroom that he had refused to let up.

She looked up at the captain, wanting to ask him something but returned to the letter.

Edgar wrote a lengthy greeting but then got to the point.

Our dear brother has departed this world. He fell sick not long after you left. Our mother could not bear his loss, and she collapsed in a monastery. I am sad to tell you that she too is on her deathbed. By the time you receive this letter, she will probably have passed on as well. I have taken this throne most apprehensively. I had not thought this was my destiny, but it seemed that God had other things in mind. I hope you are well, sister. Your other siblings are well. Ambrose is pestering me constantly to reform the church. I wish you were here so we might tease him until he leaves me alone.

He went on to say how he was hoping to keep the alliance formed between them. He would honor it on his part and wished to hear if Gorm would as well.

Thyra's hand was trembling.

She had not been expecting such news. What was she expecting, though? England had not remained in place just because she had left. It had not been dipped in amber to be preserved exactly as it was for the rest of time.

"This is such sad news you have carried, Captain."

He bowed his head as if in apology. "I am sorry to have been the one to carry it to you."

She folded the letter and handed it to Ingrid. "Please tuck this away in my room. My husband is not here at present, but I know he shall want to honor our alliance with England. You are welcome to sit and dine with us. I am assuming you are here on another mission too?"

"Yes, we are to trade in France before heading back to English soil." If the captain was put off by talking of his plans with a woman, he did not let it show. Besides, as a queen she outranked him.

"I shall ask you a favor then. Please carry back a message for King Edgar and my mother, if she still lives. It appears this will not be the case, but it would make my heart glad to think she knows I was thinking of her."

"Of course, milady." He bowed from the waist.

The men in the hall seemed interested in this show of excessive deference. She knew that they were wondering if this man was a thrall. Thyra had to bite her lip to keep herself from telling him to rise. She was becoming a woman of two lands. She would learn to navigate these different cultures one day.

She made sure that the English sailors were well fed

and looked after. No one harassed them, and she even escorted the captain to their makeshift church.

She prayed with them and after let them rest.

Her mind whirled at the thought that her oldest brother was dead and her mother was likely as well. She cursed that news couldn't reach her faster and with more regularity.

By the time Gorm returned from the borders with his warriors, the captain had sailed away, fearing to be trapped by winter storms in Denmark for the winter.

Her husband noticed her somber mood immediately and pulled her aside.

"I have done something I hope will not upset you."

"What?" His eyebrows furrowed.

"I made promises on your behalf to my brother Edgar. That you would uphold the alliance you had made with Athelstan..." She was choking on her words.

He seemed confused, but then it dawned on him. "Athelstan is dead?"

She nodded, her eyes watering from emotion. "My mother too—most likely. She is an old woman, so I wouldn't be surprised but... it still hurts and hurts all the more that I was not there to comfort them."

He pulled her into his arms. His reassuring presence soothed her. She sighed.

"I am glad you have returned."

He held her hands in his, looking down at them. He turned her hands over, examining the calluses that had formed on her fingers.

"Ursa is working you hard."

Thyra nodded, her back straightening. "You don't like it?"

"No, it's good you apply yourself. But do it because you want to, not because you have something to prove to me." He placed a kiss on her brow.

"My decisions aren't all based on you," she huffed. He laughed, seeing some of her old good humor return.

"What have I gotten myself into, Princess?"

7

_____

THWACK.

Thyra wanted to jump up and down like she had seen children do as her arrow hit the target. This was her fourth attempt at it, and it had been getting embarrassing.

"Good, you are still hesitating at the last moment," Ursa's voice sounded from behind her.

Thyra nodded. She had a tendency to second-guess herself in archery, as if she did not believe her arrow would fly straight.

When it came to fighting in a shield wall or charging at an opponent, she went as wild as any berserker. There was no stopping her. The skill of a bow and arrow was another matter entirely.

She drew another arrow from her quiver, pulled back the string on the bow, and aimed. Thyra drew in a breath, focused on the target— an old barrel padded with sawdust— then released. She fought her instinct to close her eyes at the last second.

The arrow flew straight and hit not far off from the last one.

"Better." Ursa had come up beside her. "You will have to keep practicing until you do not have to think about stopping yourself from hesitating."

Thyra nodded. She shot six more arrows before going to retrieve them. Not all of them had hit the target. Sometimes she had not accounted for the wind; other times she had been distracted. It was a learning curve, but one she wanted to master.

It had been over a year since she had come to these shores. She had adjusted in many ways. She was grateful for Gorm's encouraging presence. He provided her with more than just physical comfort. They had become true companions in every sense of the word.

Her skill with the local tongue had improved significantly. She could understand most of what was being said, and she could speak it, albeit at a slower pace than normal.

Thyra's first winter had been a shock to her. Gorm had not been kidding when he said their winters were colder than normal. She was grateful for the first time to not have windows in their room.

On the coldest of nights, they did not even bother sleeping in their own rooms and slept with everyone else in the great hall. They were like a den of sleeping bears with heavy furs and blankets layered on top of everyone.

"Shall the bear be your sigil, then?" Gorm had asked. "For you are the queen of all the bears here."

She wanted to laugh at first at the thought of such a monstrous beast as her emblem. Back in England, women usually chose emblems like fruit to represent fertility, or flowers or birds. But the more she thought about it, the more it appealed to her and she agreed.

His grandmother had approved of her decision to train in the art of war.

"It will make you strong and give you confidence. The people here respect you as Gorm's wife, but they should come to respect you for yourself as well."

Those words had stuck with Thyra. She remembered her own mother, who had at first seemed to have a decorative purpose at court. She had no real power, but over time, they had come to her for her opinion. Especially after her father had died. Thyra wanted that, but she didn't want to wait for Gorm to die to get it. Nor did she think society worked like that here.

Thyra had not insisted on them celebrating Christmas and the New Year, but she made arrangements with the priest to have special masses said. She paid for appropriate decorations to be hung around the church, attracting more visitors. Lastly, Thyra had talked to Father John about building an addition to the church that could be used to house the poor. She saw how cold it was. Even if families had a roof over their head, many could not afford enough wood to keep themselves warm throughout the season. She wanted to help where she could.

She had always felt it was the duty of rulers to oversee the well-being of their people, from the poorest to the richest.

This was something she seemed to butt heads on with Olaf. He found her little projects distasteful and distracting. His focus was on war and building up defenses. He did not want to spare people on public work projects. Nor did he like to see Thyra donating their supplies to those unfortunates.

Gorm acted as a good intermediary. He tried to placate both of them, which neither Thyra nor Olaf liked.

It seemed that Olaf preferred her when she was content to sit around with the women by the hearth all day, unable to speak to anyone.

With the approach of another winter, Thyra dreaded the long empty days sitting around. There was a festive spirit around the whole affair, but she hated being closed in. She hated that she couldn't go on walks like she was used to. Well, she had a plan in mind about what she could do to occupy her time.

She didn't say a word of it to Gorm, but she had put aside the powders from his grandmother. She wanted a child now, and what a delightful surprise it would be for Gorm.

She had not received a letter from England again, but Gorm had been keeping his word and defending the English coast from raiders to the best of his ability. He himself had not gone raiding there.

Besides Ursa, Thyra had befriended Ingrid. She

differed greatly from Thyra, a young widow only a few years older than herself, with too much love of independence to think of marrying again.

It seemed to Thyra that despite Ingrid not wanting to settle down, her bed was never empty for long either. It had shocked Thyra to learn that taking lovers casually like this was allowed. It was an open secret in England that men had dalliances, but honorable women were never to indulge themselves. They would be shunned.

There were a lot of nuances to life here that she was still learning, but she was starting to think of it as home.

———

"LADY THYRA, you must speak to Lord Gorm. It has been two years since I came to these shores and I am still in this hovel. A proper church of stone needs to be built here or the mission will fail. No wonder no one comes to pray here."

The priest was following her around the marketplace. He was barely being respectful by this point.

"I believe we are king and queen of this land. You should address us as befits our station," Thyra said, her voice icy.

"I pray to God every day, that you will see sense. If your husband does not listen to you, then you must write to the Holy Father in Rome and have him command him to do what must be done."

Thyra spun around to face him. "I see perfectly what is going on. I don't think it is surprising that no one wants to come to the church besides devout Christians. Like myself," she added pointedly.

He looked down as though he was reprimanded, but Thyra had caught the glimmer of defiance in his eye.

He was playing along only because he had to. He had no actual respect for her authority and still thought of these people as little more than barbarians. She pursed her lips together in a tight grimace.

She would pray for patience tonight. Father John was clearly unhappy here. But he didn't seem to have a plan either. If he had written to the Pope to allow for his dismissal, he hadn't said a word to her yet.

Thyra decided that after this winter, if things didn't change, she would write to the Pope herself. She didn't care how it would look. Besides, Father John was hired by her now deceased brother, Athelstan. He wouldn't be around to protest, and she doubted even he would approve of this priest.

SHE WAS WANDERING around the banks of the shoreline, climbing over the rocky terrain with her dress hiked up past her ankles. They were hunting for oysters and crawfish. Her eyes were peeled on the ground, so she was surprised when someone shouted out that they saw a boat.

Thyra straightened up, resting the basket she was holding against her hip. The sun was bright, and she squinted, shading her eyes.

There, off on the horizon she could make out the red and white sails. From the looks of it, there were four ships. Anticipation welled inside her as she thought of Gorm. These could be his ships. She waited for them to get closer.

"Should we head back, my lady?" The bells in the town were ringing, announcing the arrival of the ships too.

Thyra waited. Then she spotted the familiar carving of a dragon head on one of the ships. She released her breath. It was Gorm.

"Yes, let's go."

She was already running back up the path. It was probably not very regal of a Queen to be seen sprinting around buildings up to the docks. She tried to straighten her gown, smooth down her hair underneath her head-scarf. Thyra knew she probably smelled of fish and brine, but she figured, after days at sea, Gorm would smell worse.

It was not long before they could hear the distant sound of drums approaching. She craned her neck to get a peek at who was standing on the prow. Thyra relaxed when she recognized Gorm. Every time he left, she feared he would never return.

More people had gathered to greet the returning men. They started cheering as soon as they got close enough. The men on board waved back. It was like they were greeting conquering heroes.

The second Gorm stepped ashore, Thyra threw her arms around him.

"I am so glad to see you."

"Me too," he said. His cape was pulled tight around him. He seemed to flinch and pulled her off of him as though her weight was making him uncomfortable.

She searched his face for an explanation but saw that warning look in his eyes. Whatever it was would wait. He gave her a quick kiss and turned to the gathering crowd.

"We bring back lots of bounty from our raids. Tonight we shall celebrate!"

There was cheering, and Gorm's men began to unload the boats.

With that, Gorm wrapped his arm around her and led her home. When the crowd's attention was elsewhere, Gorm seemed to be leaning against her more. Thyra had to stop to steady herself under his unexpected weight.

"Are you well?" she asked under her breath.

He only grunted in response. Thyra assumed the answer was no.

Gorm pushed open the door to their bedroom and all but collapsed on their bed.

Thyra busied herself lighting a fire and a few candles.

As she approached the bed, she saw that the cape had fallen open. His stomach was bandaged. She recoiled, her breath a hiss as she saw that it was stained red.

"What has happened?" She rushed to his side, pulling the cape aside. He was bleeding from his side.

"What always happens when one joins in a battle."

She didn't need his sarcasm right now, but at least he was in a jolly mood. "Gorm...I'm serious."

"Sword sliced through me during a raid. Olaf stitched me up as best he could, but a day or two ago the wound reopened while I was rowing."

Thyra gaped at him. "Gorm, you can't be telling me you were rowing with a wound like this." She had started slowly peeling back the bandages to get a better look.

"You don't understand. I can't show weakness. It wasn't a bad cut. A man, I don't even remember who, came at me with the sword of a fallen comrade. I was fending off another man when he swung, but he was unused to the weapon and that was lucky for me. He sliced me, but it wasn't that deep."

"You were biting off more than you could chew," Thyra said. "You don't always have to fight in the thick of things."

"You don't know our ways then, my love."

She rolled her eyes, but concern was filling her more than anything. The gash had indeed reopened, but the skin around the wound also looked red and inflamed. This didn't look good, and she wasn't even a trained healer.

"We need to get you a doctor or someone to help you."

He shook his head. "If word got out right now, it wouldn't be good for me. Go to Olaf and ask him to bring my grandmother to me. She can help, and I trust her to not go around spreading gossip."

"We could take you to go visit her."

Gorm shook his head. "I don't think I can handle a

ride right now. But it feels good to be home. I did promise you to die in my own bed, didn't I, Thyra?"

She swatted his shoulder lightly. "I believe you also promised to live well into old age. Don't talk about dying. First things first, though. We need to clean the salt water off this wound, and these bandages are filthy."

"Whatever you want. But bring my grandmother to me. I need to rest now. It was difficult pretending all was well."

"I can imagine." Thyra was looking at him with disapproval, though he didn't catch it. He had already closed his eyes.

She pulled the blankets and furs on top of him. She would call Helga to bring in some hot water for him to bathe in. She could claim he was just tired from his journey and sleeping.

WASTING NO TIME, she went to find Olaf. He was not hard to find. If he wasn't with Gorm, he was in his work-shop, and that was exactly where she found him.

He was looking over his tools, as though making sure no one had touched them in his absence.

"You care deeply for your work. I am surprised you leave on raids," she said, speaking to him in his native tongue. He hated anything... foreign. Her included.

He grunted in agreement but did not meet her gaze. Her eyebrow rose. He sounded so much like Gorm.

"Thank you for helping my husband. I need—he

needs your help one more time. Can you go fetch his grandmother? He says she's the only one he can trust to help him right now."

Thyra wasn't sure if she had seen it correctly, but it looked as though he had shuddered. Was he afraid of the wise woman?

"She won't hurt you." She knew she should have kept her mouth shut the moment the words left her lips. He turned to her with such a furious look that she had to stop herself from taking a step back.

"I am not afraid."

"Good, then you won't mind leaving now? I am worried about Gorm."

"He will be fine."

"I am sure he will be if you bring his grandmother," Thyra pressed, not willing to give way to this man.

He turned away, grabbing a heavy cloak from a hook on the wall. "Fine."

"Thank you," she said, her voice softening. "I appreciate it."

"I don't do it for you."

"I know that." Her original ire at him returned just as soon as it had gone.

She watched him leave, feeling foolish just standing there. How long would it take for them to return? His grandmother was surely too old to travel by horseback. Usually, she came by wagon. A passing farmer would give her passage on his trip into town, usually in exchange for a charm.

There was no time to dwell on that now. She

returned to Gorm's side, taking the hot steaming jug of water from Helga's hands.

"I'll tend to my husband. It's been so long since I have seen him."

A knowing smile flashed across Helga's face. "I'll make sure you aren't disturbed, milady."

"Thank you. Enjoy the celebrations tonight. Hopefully, we will feel up to joining you all." Thyra forced herself to smile and press down her worry.

The fire was still burning, but the candle had burned out. Thyra lit another, holding it over Gorm's face. He looked pale, but she couldn't see very well in this dim light.

"Husband?" She pulled up a stool beside the bed. "Are you sleeping?"

"I was," came the gruff reply. "It hurts. I don't like admitting it, but it does. Curse my foolish pride."

"Yes, I wish you'd let me call a doctor. Then you could be tended to here and now."

He shook his head, the trinkets in his hair twinkling as they hit against each other.

She touched his forehead with the back of her hand, checking for fever as her mother used to do for them. "Well, at least you don't feel warm. I'm going to clean the wound."

"Give me some wine first," he said, speaking in half gasps.

"There's wine in here?"

"I stashed some in here before I left. I don't trust

those servants looking after the storerooms. I seem to have to buy wine all too often."

Thyra chided him. "That's probably because you drink it too often, and when you are drunk, you become very generous."

"Do I really?"

She nodded, lifting his shirt gingerly. She didn't want to hurt him if the blood had caked the shirt on to the skin.

"Let's get this off of you first. If you weren't injured, I would have thrown you into the river, you smell so bad."

He chuckled. "You sure know how to flatter a man."

She dabbed at the wound with the hot water. Gorm's sharp intake of breath was the only sound he made as she did so. She started using clean linen to clean around the wound better. There was a time when this would have made her squeamish, but after learning to butcher animals in her brother's kitchens, she had gotten used to it. Still, she had never envisioned herself doing this.

It appeared the cut had indeed been made cleanly. Gorm was lucky it wasn't some rusty axe that the man had picked up.

At last she managed to clean the area. The skin was scrubbed pink and raw, and any sign of dirt, dried blood, or salt was gone.

She didn't know what she should do for the wound, as she didn't have proper bandages to use to wrap around his torso, and she wanted to just wait for Olaf to return. She used their sheet to wrap up his chest tight. The wound was not seeping blood now that he was resting.

"I should get up and go to the hall," Gorm said into the silence of the room. Only the crackling of the log on the fire could be heard.

"You will do no such thing. It doesn't seem so bad now, but I bet it will start bleeding again if you try to sit up. I don't want to bury my husband after just a year."

"It's good to know you think so highly of me." He reached out a hand for her. She took it and he pulled her toward him. "If I do, I shall be happy to die in your arms."

She pulled away with a laugh. "You are assuming I would stick around to witness such foolishness. Why won't you let me call for a doctor?"

"My kingdom is newly formed. This bit of bad luck, well... it could prove to be my undoing. I trust my men with my life, but gossip would spread. Those lords who constantly test my strength would choose now to attack, and I can't have that. They won't follow me if they think I'm weak or that the gods have turned their backs to me."

She shook her head in frustration. Thyra couldn't wrap her head around it.

"Besides, think of the Germans to the south. They are sure to hear about it too, and then they would be more than happy to press for war now."

Thyra bit her lower lip. Now was not the time to argue with him. They could always be attacked. He was often gone for weeks out raiding. What would stop anyone from attacking then? Or his lords from rebelling against him?

She looked up at the ceiling, praying to the overhead timbers for patience.

Thyra made the excuse of going out to get them food as a way of distracting herself.

Her appearance in the great hall did not go unnoticed, and they called for her to bring out Gorm. She had to make some bawdy jests about how he was too tired and she too eager to let him leave their bed. They were too drunk and in too good of a mood to mind. Many of the sailors had fallen asleep, their hands still on their tankards.

She fed Gorm herself, not wanting him to sit up. She had grabbed some porridge and venison for him. She ripped the pieces of meat apart with her fingers so it would be easier for him to chew and not choke.

"I feel as though I am a babe."

"I won't hear any complaint from you right now. Next time, just don't get injured."

"I'll keep that in mind." His voice was a low growl.

It was well into the evening when the door to their room was opened.

Gorm's grandmother stepped through. She was a small woman and barely had to open the door to get in.

She was wrapped in a dark cloak and hid a bag underneath it.

"Where is Olaf?" Gorm asked her.

"You drag me here in the middle of the night and you ask about that man?" She clicked her tongue in displeasure. "He is at home. He thought it would be too conspicuous if he came in too."

Thyra was secretly glad he had not come. It would

feel like an invasion of her space to have him in here. Even though he had helped her husband.

"Well, let me see what you've done to yourself."

"I tried to clean the wound as best I could," Thyra began, looking apprehensive. She didn't want Olga to disapprove of her.

"I'm sure you did, dear. Sit by my side and I will show you how to tend wounds like these for the next time."

Thyra gulped. She realized she had been foolish to assume this would not be a common occurrence. Her husband's business was war. Of course he would get hurt. He wasn't some invincible Hercules.

His grandmother pressed against the wound as if testing the flesh and seeing how Gorm reacted.

"I will cauterize it. It will hurt, but I don't think stitches will do much here. The man didn't cut you that deep, but unfortunately, it is also hard to keep this area still."

She handed Thyra a long thin dagger. "Stick it into the fire until it turns red hot, or you feel you can't hold it anymore."

Thyra did as she was told. As she held it there, she heard Olga start chanting, her voice low but powerful.

Her fingers were beginning to hurt and the heat was growing intolerable, but she merely tightened her grip on the blade. She would keep it in the fire for as long as she could.

"That will be enough. Bring it here."

The chanting had stopped.

Thyra handed over the dagger. She saw Gorm was biting down on a piece of leather.

"I will count to three." He nodded. "Okay. One…" And Olga placed the hot dagger over the wound.

The smell of burning flesh was intolerable. Gorm groaned in pain, despite his best attempts at keeping quiet.

Then, all in a moment it was over. The wound was no longer gaping open but sealed by the burned flesh.

"This will help knit your skin back together," his grandmother said, unfazed. Even as Gorm was still trying his best to keep from screaming out in pain. His chest heaved, and he looked like he might throw up.

Thyra regretted giving him food to eat.

She watched as his grandmother rubbed a paste over the wound, and then she helped bandage him up.

"You shouldn't move until morning," she said. "Then be careful, especially lifting your left hand or bending at the waist. If it bleeds again, we shall have to start all over again, and I'm sure you don't want that."

Gorm nodded through gritted teeth, still too on edge to speak.

Thyra thanked her. Relieved that she didn't seem to think it was anything serious.

"Well, I shall go find somewhere to sleep. You might as well burn these rags." She made a sweeping motion over his old shirt and the makeshift bandages that had been used. "Throw this into the fire after you are done. It will give you both peaceful sleep."

Thyra was handed a pouch of herbs. She could smell the lavender.

"Well, sleep well. May Freya watch over you."

They were alone again. Thyra felt more relaxed but tentative about approaching Gorm, so she busied herself with doing what his grandmother had said.

The lavender burned sweetly, filling her nose with a fresh scent different from that of burning flesh. A smell she would never forget.

"How are you?" she said at last, taking his hand.

"I will live," he said. "I have survived worse. It was just a shock. Never listen to her when she says she will count to three. She never does."

Thyra chuckled, glad to see his spirits were somewhat improved if he could joke.

IF ANYONE THOUGHT anything was amiss, they didn't say anything. Gorm was a good actor, never showing anyone the pain he was in. They took the sudden appearance of his grandmother the next day as a peculiarity to be ignored. After all, she was a wise woman not constrained by reason, and the harvest would be upon them soon.

Thyra went about her day as normally as possible, trying not to look concerned for her husband every time he rode out or went to help with some physical task.

The wound stayed closed and it hurt him less with each passing week. She knew he was healed when he turned to her one night, pulling her close, and kissed the crook of her neck.

She welcomed his attention. Her worry dissipated into the background as her desire for him grew.

By the time the harvest came around, he was well enough to perform his duties without fear he might stumble.

She watched as he sacrificed a cow in the temple of his gods so they would bless this harvest. Everyone who could be spared came to witness the ceremony. The priest collected the draining blood from the animal and said a prayer over it. She looked away for most of the ceremony, finding it distasteful. She had not taken part actively, but she accepted the mark her husband drew on her forehead with the blood of the animal. The meat was prepared by the priests and shared among all attendants. Music started up and Gorm pulled her onto the dance floor. They lost themselves in the drumming and excitement. Caught up in the moment, she joined everyone in a toast to Odin.

Father John had a few choice words for her the next day. She resolved then and there that she would write to the Pope. Father John would never respect her, nor would he act as a good spiritual guide for her.

The autumn equinox was over, and now, besides the rush to get everything in for the harvest and build up winter stores, there was nothing left to do out in the fields.

Still, the days were busy. Clothes needed to be made or mended, ale brewed, bread kneaded. Buildings needed to be repaired. Meat had to be smoked and fish salted. If they did not prepare enough, then it would be a lean winter and an even hungrier spring. She went out every morning to pick berries with the other women. They had to venture farther and farther afield, as the ones close to home had been picked clean. They went in groups, fearing bears, which were in an eating frenzy this time of year.

Soon Thyra was learning how to prepare for the yule celebration. The men had cut the logs, but it was the women who arranged the herbs on the great logs. She had helped pick the holly and the cranberries to decorate them. They would burn for three days and nights, filling the halls with sweet-smelling herbs.

She watched as the men prepared a great wheel. Last year, she had witnessed it being lit on fire and rolled down a hill. It was to signify the return of the sun after the dark winter months. She had not quite understood it then. Now she appreciated the intricate carvings and runes they carved into the wooden beams.

Pictures of wolves and Thor's hammer danced across the wood next to the great snake that was to devour itself and the world along with it.

The marketplace was now empty. Thyra was lucky she had lots to do to keep herself busy. She tried to keep his grandmother company too. Now that Gorm was healed and out of danger, she liked to comment that he had gotten himself injured on purpose just to pull her away from her work.

"You would have had to come anyway. You can't live on your own in winter."

"What are you saying, girl?" his grandmother said, her eyes flashing angrily. "I am stronger than you, that's for sure. Everyone seems to think that just because I am old I cannot manage to do anything. Well, listen to me. I don't need to be treated like some child."

"Grandmother, come along. I didn't mean it like that." Thyra sighed. She was exasperated with the opinionated woman. It seemed she couldn't say anything right to her. She could see why she preferred it out in the woods. "I promise I won't pester you anymore. If you need something to do, come find me. Otherwise I won't bother you."

"Good," Olga said with a sharp nod. She gave Thyra's hand a squeeze. Then she stopped, as if something had frozen her still. That direct gaze of hers was turned on Thyra, but she said nothing, and not wishing to say something to upset her Thyra didn't ask what was happening.

Thyra didn't have long to dwell on his grandmother's strangeness. She was a peculiar woman but also powerful, and she wanted to stay on her good side.

She was working with Ingrid and Frejis to check the stores of the fermenting hops. They would turn into a potent wine. Thyra couldn't stomach it and never drank it. She preferred the mulled ale or wine. For yule, they would need enough to last them for three days. People invited usually brought their own food. Even a wealthy household like their own could not afford to feed and house hundreds of people for so many days.

Thyra had taken it upon herself to walk to the church despite the frost on the ground.

She prayed on her knees for Gorm's safety and thanked God for the health and prosperity she enjoyed. By now, she ignored the priest, and he performed his duties mechanically. She missed the Christmas celebrations they would have back in England and how the choir would sing so beautifully. The church here would be silent.

"You should come celebrate yule with us. At the very least, you would have a few days of good eating, and perhaps you wouldn't be so lonely," she suggested, keeping her tone light and friendly.

He scoffed. "I would not celebrate some pagan ritual with heathens."

"Come for the food. There's no need to celebrate with them if you find it so distasteful." She wanted to wipe the sneer off his face.

"I would be witness to it, and that's just as bad. Don't think God isn't watching you," he said, distaste dripping from every word.

She frowned but said nothing, just left. Did he not realize she was one of the only reasons he had food and wood for the winter? But she wouldn't complain over semantics. She would find herself another priest and he would be recalled to Rome or England. She didn't particularly care. She could respect him for the vows he took, but she did not care for him as a person.

Back at home, she tried to forget about him. She hated that he could always get a rise out of her. Now she was sitting by the hearth, her feet propped up on a stone to be warmed by the fire.

"You will join us for Mōdraniht," a voice said from behind her.

She turned her head and saw Gorm's grandmother standing behind her with Helga at her side.

"What is that?"

Olga grinned. "You will see. A festival just for women. After the night of yuletide. We celebrate the goddesses and the Norns who've governed our fates. Mothers of us all."

Was it Thyra's imagination, or did she linger over the word *mother*? But she nodded, happy to be included. She didn't even ask why last year she had not been.

More and more people poured into the city. From the highest rungs of society to the lowest, they came with their goods and as much food as they could carry. This would be one of the last times that people would gather for the season. No one with any sense would risk a long journey in the middle of winter unless it was necessary.

Thyra still felt very much like an outsider looking in. She didn't quite feel included, nor did she know many people. However, one thing she enjoyed was having Gorm around more.

He was a peacemaker— always handling disputes between people as calmly as possible. Often she sat beside him on his dais, in a chair on his right-hand side, and watched the proceedings.

"The goat he sold me had a lame foot. Hardly a

worthy sacrifice to Odin," a man with a beard so large it overtook his face said.

"It was not lame when I sold it to him. He must not have taken care of it," another retorted.

Thyra watched Gorm make a great show of deliberating.

"Have either of you any witnesses?"

"My wife," the seller said.

"That is hardly an impartial witness," the bearded man said.

Gorm sighed. "Enough. We are here to celebrate yuletide. Since there are no witnesses and you both have good honest characters, I will take the lame goat and you may have one of mine, in exchange for one silver piece." The other people listening around the hall shouted their assent.

The bearded man bowed at the waist. "Most generous." Though it was clear he was still grumbling about it.

Thyra looked over at him. "Why take the lame goat?"

Gorm gave her a half smile. "It is simple: winter is approaching, and we can never have enough food. We have our sacrifice to Odin prepared, but that man, Harlfar, did not. He would have to travel all the way back to his farm to fetch another animal. So why not make everyone happy in some way? I would never have gotten such a good bargain otherwise. To me, it doesn't matter if the goat we slaughter for the winter is lame or not. But Odin would care."

"I don't think Harlfar is thrilled though," she pointed out.

"He'll come around. He probably would have given me that solid gold brooch he was wearing to make sure he wouldn't have to make the trip back or miss out on making an offering to Odin this year."

Thyra nodded. "Well, at the very least, no one's reputation was ruined. Who do you think was right?"

Gorm shrugged. "Only two people know the truth of it. I couldn't know."

"But if you had to place a wager?" Thyra said, her grin spreading wider as she tried to wheedle an answer out of him.

"Who would you have thought was in the right?" He turned the question back around on her.

"I don't know them well enough to make a judgment."

"I do not either, but even if I did, then my decision would be biased."

"So you settled for the middle ground, where you found some way to profit?" Thyra said, now having to chuckle to herself.

"Of course."

He had leaned over to her to whisper this last part. His breath sent goose bumps spreading over the nape of her neck.

"Perhaps you could seek an audience with me too," he said. "Maybe one in private?"

Feeling playful, she nudged him away from her. "I am afraid I could not pull you away from your duties at such a time."

"You are wrong, wife. You'd find me quite

amenable."

She turned her head away, pretending he had not gotten a rise out of her. She knew him better now to know that he was merely playing games. Thyra had still not developed that wonderful skill of holding back her feelings. Someone could always see what she was thinking just by looking at her face.

The next few days were spent making decorations to hang around the hall and on the outside of buildings. Despite the chill, she worked with everyone else with a merry spirit. At one point, she even helped make tallow, but when Gorm threatened to have her thrown into the river because she came into their room smelling so bad, she desisted.

The festive spirit full of anticipation was cut short by clamoring in the middle of the night.

Gorm shot to his feet, reaching for a sword and an axe. He had not even dressed properly before he was out the door.

Thyra's own heart was pounding in her chest. She had not thought anything of it. She had heard the noises but thought it was some drunken brawl and was ready to go back to bed when Gorm had sprung up.

This seemed serious, not to mention dangerous. Instead of pulling the covers over her and hiding under the warm comfort they provided, she got out of bed. She pulled on a pair of leggings she usually kept for training and got up, grabbing a small axe they used for chopping firewood. She knew enough by now to use it with some efficiency.

Tossing a fur-lined cloak over her and grabbing one for Gorm, she stepped outside their darkened room.

There were shouts coming from the great hall, but it did not sound like a battle. Still cautious, she peeked around the corner to see.

Gorm was shouting to the half-asleep men. Shouting for them to hurry.

Beds were tossed aside, people were getting dressed. Thyra saw the fear on the women's faces as well as the confusion.

She touched Gorm's shoulder.

"What is it?" she said, her voice tentative.

"There's been an attack. The Germans have raided our southern borders. That man there stumbled in here half-frozen in the night. Calling for help. We thought we were under attack. I am sorry if I frightened you."

"I am fine," she said, glad she hadn't running into the room holding an axe above her head like some wild animal. "Where are you going?"

"We must go beat them back. Show them that even now, in winter, we cannot be meddled with," he said. "Besides, those are my people and I am their liege. It is my duty to defend them."

She nodded, but Thyra was biting her tongue to keep herself from telling him not to go. They were finally getting to spend more time together. "First, you should probably dress."

Gorm looked down at his bare legs and laughed. "Why, so you are right, Princess."

"Can you not just fight them back once and for all?" She asked.

"How do you propose I do that?" He said, while fighting with his belt buckle.

She was silent then said the next thing that came to her. "Just fortify your realm with a wall so big none would dare attack us."

His lips twitched as if wanting to smile but he was too focused on the task ahead.

She watched him leave. Everyone was on edge. The band of men were all on horseback, barely any supplies with them in their haste to leave. But they were armed to the teeth, their eyes filled with fury and anger. She would not wish to meet them on the road.

With Gorm and most of the able-bodied men gone, the great hall and town felt strangely empty. He had not left them defenseless and had even instructed Olaf to stay behind.

That was clearly not what Olaf had intended, but it was a great honor that Gorm was willing to trust him so much.

"You shall have the rule of the city while I am gone," Gorm had told her as he jumped into the saddle. "Take care of my people."

Those were traditional words of parting whenever a lord went out to battle. Thyra didn't like it one bit. She hated that her heart was gripped with fear.

She busied herself, helping the others clear the hall. Judging from the night sky, it was nearly dawn. There was no sense returning to bed.

Everyone moved at a sluggish pace.

After a hot bowl of porridge, she walked the edge of the city with a piece of bread and cold meat in her hands. She could see her breath as. The heavy cloak did little to fend off the cold that seemed to penetrate deep in her bones.

She got to the front gate and noticed it had been left open. She froze and looked around for the guards that were supposed to be stationed here.

Gorm always ordered the city gates closed at night. Perhaps they thought since it was day they could leave them open. But where were the guards?

She would order them closed. She didn't feel safe, even if the raiders were far south and Gorm was riding out to meet them.

She headed back to the hall with growing apprehension blossoming in her as she thought about it. Without realizing it, she was half running by this point. The streets were deserted, which wasn't odd considering the cold and how early it was. Many people were probably still eating in the hall or sleeping in their beds.

She stumbled into Olaf just then. He was talking to a trio of men and she rushed over. Not taking his feelings into consideration when she interrupted whatever they were talking about.

"The gates should be closed," Thyra said through panting breaths. She was still unable to form her thoughts properly.

He rolled his eyes at her and looked ready to dismiss her.

"Why were they left open?" She had collected herself at this point.

He was taken aback by her accusation. "You are wrong. They were ordered to be closed once the king rode out."

"They aren't now."

Olaf had always been pale, but now he went paler still. He swore under his breath and grabbed the man closest to him by his cloak.

"Go gather all the men and weapons you can. We will meet in the market square."

"The gates? Shouldn't we close them?"

He swung round to face her.

"We will be dead men if we try now."

Thyra put a hand to her chest. "What are you saying?"

"We are under attack. If they have not snuck into the city already, they will soon be here. Most likely they are waiting for us to shoot us down. We must sound the alarm, mount a defense."

If this was any other time, she would be honored he was even taking the time to communicate with her. Then she realized he was telling her this not because he'd decided they should be best friends now, but because she would have to be seen giving out the orders. She was the de facto ruler.

Her hand touched the rudimentary axe tied to her belt. He followed her motion.

"Yes, even you may have to fight."

People were panicking. They shouted and knocked

on all the doors as they passed. Anyone inside was soon scrambling up, women and children running to the great hall.

This was wrong. Thyra didn't like that they were all gathering in one place. Someone needed to ride out to warn Gorm to come back. What if he had been ambushed on the road? She pushed down the thought.

There were only a handful of fighting men available to them. They tried to barricade some of the city streets leading up to the great hall.

She didn't speak much more to Olaf. Let him try to organize the men. She ran inside to the people gathered around the stone hearth.

She ordered them as calmly as she could to pack as much as they could carry and dress warmly. If this wasn't just a random band of raiders, they would have to flee. Firewood, food, this all would have to be carried.

Thyra looked to Gorm's grandmother. What would she do? Could she run if she had to?

People were scrambling all around her as she tried to give directions and keep people calm. She knew two things: one was that they had to be prepared to run, and two was that they needed to keep steady heads on their shoulders. They would have a better chance working together than everyone going off panicking in all directions.

She remembered Ursa telling her how often in the heat of the battle, fear could overtake even the toughest soldiers and they would be dead men after that. Fear made you make mistakes just as overconfidence did.

She saw Olaf step into the chaos that encompassed the walls. Their eyes met across the room. Thyra, deciding that this was not the time to argue over precedence, walked over to him.

"Yes?"

"I have sent scouts, one or two men to see if they can find anything. We think they are waiting outside the city gates, but they must have a man inside. I don't know how many there are." He took a moment to look around. "You are planning on having them move out?"

"Yes, we go by the docks. There is a path. We can follow the shore and leave by that way," she said.

"It is a treacherous way. There will be ice and the wind to contend with."

Thyra didn't appreciate that he was looking at her like she was a fool.

"Do you suggest that I leave out the gates? We would be exposed and out in the open if we went any other way. The beach would give us the most cover among the crags and rocks."

"Well, you may not have to leave," he said. "This could be nothing more than a few people causing trouble. I'll skin them alive myself when I get ahold of them."

"I hope you are right, but if you are wrong, you and your men will need to retreat. Shall I wait for you to give the signal to leave?"

He opened his mouth to reply, but the tolling of bells in the city drowned out his words.

"You may have to leave now. I'll be right back."

There was more panic now than ever. The air was heavy with it. Thyra felt as though she couldn't think.

"Everyone, please listen," she tried to say, but to no avail. "Quiet!" she shouted at last. "We don't know what will happen, but prepare to leave and we will go down by the beach. It is important we stick together. Carry as much food and necessities as you dare."

The crowd stilled, then sprang into action. Moving with purpose now. Ursa appeared at Thyra's side, dressed in warrior garb. Three other women Thyra recognized from training were with her.

"We shall stay and fight here," Ursa said, a hand on the hilt of her sword.

Thyra shook her head. "These people will need your protection, though hopefully it won't come to that."

Ursa frowned. "We shall not run like cowards."

"Is that what you think I am doing? Gorm entrusted me with safeguarding his people."

"This is our way. We fight and defend what is ours."

"Am I not your queen? I made an oath that I would lay down my life defending this country," Thyra shot back, just as heated as Ursa. She took a step forward. "If there are too many of them, we will get slaughtered here. We need to survive and somehow get word to Gorm that we need his help. If we all die here, then Gorm will return to a trap. I will not see my husband killed for my foolishness. I cannot force you to go, but I hope you will."

Ursa hesitated now as she considered her words. "Very well. I see that you have a point. We will stay, but if we see the tide going against us we will retreat."

"Live to fight another day," Thyra said, a quip Ursa had always thrown at her. Her teacher smiled back ruefully.

Olaf returned, his face grave. "There are many of them. At least thirty by my estimation. This is no band traveling by accident. This was planned. They are moving in. The bells have made them cautious. They weren't expecting anyone to be around to witness their coming. They are probably looking to pilfer as much and as fast as they can." He cursed again.

Looking around, Thyra could imagine what he was thinking. There was a lot of pilfering to be had here, in goods but also in women.

"We need to leave. We all need to leave," Thyra said, breaking the silence. "You have what, ten men? It is not enough. Fourteen with Ursa's crew."

"They would be upon us in the blink of an eye if we did not mount a defense." Olaf looked frustrated with her.

"A diversion, then? Can you think of anything that could stall them? Or at least keep them off our trail so we can get away. They might be happy enough when they see everything they can plunder."

"We don't have time for this. Leave now." Olaf all but commanded.

Thyra bit her lip. "We station archers along the buildings. They would have easy targets and it would force the invaders be more cautious in their approach. We slowly retreat and leave them the open hall...they would be tempted by the open doors but fear that it is a

206

trap. We can set fire to the square, trapping them around it. They would be distracted enough with that and trying to get their plunder. They would think we abandoned the city to them."

Ursa nodded. "It could work. They might decide it is not worth their time to chase after us. They know with winter it would be easy to chase us down or that we would even come crawling back for the safety of our homes. Let them get drunk on our ale and wine."

"Drunk on poison," a voice from behind the three interjected. In her hand, a small glass jar. "We add this to the ale we just happened to leave lying around. Hopefully, they will be foolish enough to drink it. Then we won't even need my son's return to save us."

"Grandmother, that's brilliant."

Olaf frowned, looking from one woman to another. They outnumbered him three to one. "This is madness."

"It's strategy and an order," Thyra said, squaring her shoulders back.

"Very well," he said, knowing there was little time to lose. "If we die, it is on your shoulders, not mine."

He turned to leave, but Thyra grabbed his arm. She saw him flinch at the contact, but she pulled him aside to the alcove.

"I have a special request of you." She took a deep breath. "I charge you with finding my husband and warning him of what has befallen us here."

Olaf shook his head. "I was put in command here."

"Command of our defenses. I am queen," Thyra said, finally claiming the title with more seriousness than ever. "I will die here if it is what the gods will, but you will not. You will ride and warn my husband and bring him back to our defense. If we do manage to escape, then we will be facing the elements and are likely to perish unless we can somehow defeat these men. You are the only one I know who could survive the trek."

She didn't know why he didn't fight her on this, but at last he nodded.

"I'll slip away the minute I can."

"We need to put aside our differences and work together for now."

He agreed. "Very well."

She bowed her head in thanks and left him to get on with it.

Now that they had a purpose and a plan, they moved like clockwork. Grandmother wanted to stay behind. Either to hide or make a stand.

"I would like to see which of them would dare strike down a sorceress of my caliber."

But Thyra wouldn't hear of it. "I shall have you carried out of here."

It took two of Ursa's warriors to hold her. Working together, they would carry her on their backs. Children too young to make the journey would have to be carried. It would be a hard march, but she figured if they could make it to the woods past the shore, then they could find shelter among the trees.

The gods smiled on them that day. Their plan went off as well as might have been expected, considering it was haphazardly thrown together. They had suffered losses, but a larger crisis was averted.

Thyra watched as Olaf broke away from the group, leading an old mare by the reins. It looked like it would collapse just as soon as it would run. Once he had gotten out of sight, he would mount and ride as fast as he could to reach Gorm and the main army. Thyra said a silent prayer, hoping some divine being would help the horse last the journey.

Not all the men that created the diversion had returned. Thyra had to push back the horror of being indirectly responsible for their deaths, if they were dead. Looking at their ragtag group, she could tell that if Gorm did not return soon, there would be more deaths laid at her door. Still, this was a better alternative to certain slaughter in the city. Even if they had stayed and tried to hold down their positions, all it would take was for the group of attackers to set fire to their houses and fortifications. They would be burned alive in their wooden buildings.

She had to keep repeating to herself that she had made the right choice. It was getting hard to do as the cold started setting in and the adrenaline was leaving her system. They needed some sort of shelter. She didn't want to risk a fire right now. But if they had to sleep out here overnight...

Their inaction was causing people to start to panic as their anxiety got the better of them. They were sitting ducks out here. Many turned to her for guidance but she had to think.

"Child, we must head for my home in the woods. I have supplies there. It is a holy place that I doubt even these raiders would dare attack. I can't fit everyone in that old hovel of mine, but even those who would have to stay outside would find it warmer there. I am protected on two sides by mountains," Olga said as though reading her thoughts. Her initial displeasure at having been dragged away was gone.

"Gorm might return today. He will have taken back the city."

"If you think we can risk that, then we stay."

Thyra bit her lip. "It would be a long journey on foot."

"It would be more dangerous to stay here. You said it yourself."

"Yes, we can't stay in one place for long. At least when we are on the move, we might not notice the cold either."

She announced to them the plan. The promise of building up a good fire and food stores gave everyone energy to press on after a short break.

Whatever food they had managed to grab would be all they could assume they might get their hands on. How long would this last? A day or two at most? They only had one or two pack animals.

The soldiers looked to her for direction, and she sent one ahead to scout the area and make sure the path was passable. The other three she asked to bring up the rear to ensure no one was going to attack them from behind.

Thyra looked at the tired face of a child no older than six or seven.

Her throat tightened in discomfort and anxiety. She was trying to reassure herself that this was the best she could do for them. If she could, she would lay down her life for them, but that would accomplish nothing.

They walked in silence. Only the sound of their boots crunching on snow and ice echoed around them. The steam of their breath rose in the air. They moved slower now, making sure everyone was getting the help they needed.

Thyra tried not to think of the provisions they had left behind. She tried her best not to think of what could have been if she had made different decisions. It would be a waste of energy to dwell on what-ifs.

They spent two nights holed up at Olga's home. Snow was cleared and a large bonfire was built up. They pulled material and heavy clothes from inside, making patchwork tents and canopies to protect themselves from the elements as best they could. The children and elderly slept inside, piled one on top of the other it had seemed.

Thyra had been surprised by how many had refused to take the comfort of the hovel, pushing others to take it instead.

She commented on this to Ursa, who had merely shrugged.

"It is the way we do things. It doesn't help that we are stubborn and don't want to show our weakness," she said. "There are very few people who would actually prefer sleeping outside in winter."

From the low timbre of her voice, Thyra could tell Ursa was exhausted.

The men were still standoffish with her, but Thyra admired the respect they showed to Grandmother. Olaf seemed to have been the de facto leader when Gorm was gone, so she didn't hold it against them.

That night, when she crawled onto her makeshift pallet on the cold hard ground, she began to pray as she did every night when her heart seized. Father John. Where was he? She shot up, looking around, her eyes wide, desperate to find him among the people here. It was hard to tell among the furs and blankets, the huddled forms of people.

She couldn't see him. Maybe he was inside Grandmother's hut. Maybe he was one of the indiscernible figures. Maybe he had been left behind.

She tried to rack her brain. They had alerted as many people as they could about the impending attack. Her spirits fell as she realized that not everyone could have been accounted for. Maybe many had chosen to flee the scene. Maybe some had chosen to stay and fight or hide away in their homes.

There had not been time. Damn Father John's stubborn pride and insistence on not associating with pagans.

Thyra thought of all the times she had wished him gone from these shores. If he died, was it because she had ill-wished him? Wave after wave of guilt hit her, and she began trembling.

Ingrid, who was sleeping by her side, woke and seeing her looking so ill hopped to her aid.

"Shall I fetch Olga? What is wrong?" She was groggy and tired herself, but Thyra's fear and anxiety was affecting her too.

"I-I can't... there's so much I didn't..." Thyra couldn't form a coherent thought. She was dumbstruck by her inadequacy.

Vaguely, she remembered Ingrid rising to her feet, but the next moment Olga was crouched down at her side, chanting and waving a charm over her, pouring something down her throat, urging her to swallow.

Whatever it was seemed to light her on fire. Warmth spread from her belly outward, until the tingling seemed to have reached her very fingertips.

Her eyes focused on Olga's worried expression.

"Breathe. Take a deep breath."

She listened and was relieved as the weight pressing down on her chest seemed to lift.

"Freya protect you. Thor give you strength..."

She could understand the prayer being said over the cup in Olga's hand. She drank deep.

"Finish the whole cup," came the instruction, and she obliged.

Thyra felt steady again. Her heartbeat regulated, and though her head pounded, she could think clearly again. She tried to assure them she was fine, but her voice cracked as she spoke.

"I don't think this is everyone. Father John might have been left behind. Who knows how many other people? I have failed everyone."

"Hush, child. Don't even think such a foolish thing."

"But it is true."

"You did the best you could. You are inexperienced, that is true. But even those who've seen more winters than you have faltered. Not everyone can be saved. You cannot let yourself be overwhelmed by guilt."

Thyra heard her words and knew they were true. Life was unpredictable. God took with one hand what he gave with another. Still, she didn't know if she could forgive herself. How else would God punish her now for her sins? Especially toward Father John.

"I want you to sleep now. We need you here. We need you thinking clearly."

Olga's words were a command. Thyra was eager to obey. It was harder to lead than to follow. She was learning that now. She remembered her lessons on Plato and how he had always said ignorance was bliss. How true that was. What she wouldn't give right now to change places with that child she had seen earlier.

THE NEXT DAY she felt better, but her feet felt heavy and her brain sluggish.

Grandmother instructed them to drag out an enormous cauldron of metal from her hut. They cooked soup on the fire. The delicious scent of boiling onions, herbs, and meat filled the air and made all their mouths water. Some of the soldiers had gone hunting and brought back a rabbit and a handful of game birds. It wasn't much. There were over twenty hungry mouths to feed. But added to the soup and the other odds and ends they had, everyone's bellies were full one way or another.

Thyra didn't want to think about what would happen if they had to stay here longer. They would have a better chance if they fragmented and made for some nearby farms. Such a journey would last days and would likely lead to them freezing to death in the cold, but what else could they do?

Luckily, the next morning, one of the soldiers came running into the camp, shouting that King Gorm was approaching.

Thyra ran forward down the now familiar path to the entrance of Grandmother's land. She waited at the gate between those two skulls, her eyes not moving from the road ahead.

She ran forward when she saw Gorm at the head of his troop. Relief filled her with such joy. He had barely jumped down from his horse when she sprang into his arms, tears streaming down her face.

"I am so happy to see you, Gorm."

"And I you, Thyra."

They held each other a moment longer, Thyra drinking in the comfort of his strong arms and warm body. They separated and Thyra's eyes met Olaf's. He nodded his head toward her in greeting. More respectful acknowledgement than she had ever received.

Gorm walked at her side into the heart of the camp and announced that he and his men had made the city safe once again. They were here to escort them home.

Cheers went up. The camp began packing up.

Gorm greeted his grandmother personally, kneeling at her feet for her blessing. Thyra did not hear what he said to her, but she was sure he was also asking for forgiveness.

The trek back home took longer. Fear was no longer driving them forward, and though everyone was eager to be home again and warm by their hearths, they were on the verge of collapsing.

That night, Gorm held her as she cried. She wept from gratitude, from exhaustion, from everything and nothing.

He seemed to understand what she needed, and he listened to everything she had to say, not complaining that his night shift was being ruined by her tears.

"My people are grateful to you. Olaf is as well, whether he shows it or not. Many more people would have died if you had not ordered them out of the city," he said to reassure her.

Thyra nodded and tried to keep herself from objecting. She had not been prepared. She should have been more careful. So many things.

"If anything, I am to blame. I usually don't act so hastily, but all I could think of was dealing with the issue and returning to my wife, who had ordered me to build her a wall." His casual joke got a chuckle out of her.

"So what happened?"

"There were some troublemakers on the road. We were eager to press on since we had encountered a small ambush, fearing this was a scouting party. We pushed our horses hard, but then we heard someone riding up behind us. It was Olaf, of all people, and I knew the moment I saw him that we were riding in the wrong direction. I feared I would return to find you dead. You should have seen me then. All cowered in the face of my anger. When we stormed the city, I went mad with rage. They will call me berserker now, even though I have not earned the title."

She listened with rapt attention as he told her how they had snuck into the city and attacked the men. The invaders had not expected such swift retaliation. They were busy getting drunk on wine or ale and eating as much as they could. Gold and other loot had been gathered in the main hall. Some of the men had already died, discovering too late that the ale left behind had been poisoned.

Thyra grinned, imagining the satisfaction his grandmother would have upon hearing that.

They slept in each other's arms that night, neither daring to let go of the other. Thyra had unburdened herself to him, but her guilt had not magically disappeared. She knew it would haunt her for the rest of her days.

They had found Father John dead behind his altar. She saw to it that he would be given a Christian burial. She read the prayer herself, knowing that he would hate this more than anything, but promised to have a proper priest come and consecrate his grave. Masses would be said for his soul, and hopefully he would find peace in the afterlife.

The raiders had caused a lot of damage, destroying or

killing what they could not have taken with them. Only luck had prevented the whole city from being set aflame. Some of the storehouses had been affected, and they were now going to have to be more careful than ever with their food supplies.

Gorm ordered hunting parties to go out immediately, while the weather made the terrain still traversable.

Funerals were held, and sacrifices made to the gods.

Life went on in more ways than one...

"You cannot be serious." Gorm's deep voice echoed through the chamber. "Tell me now this is some jest you and my grandmother have concocted."

Thyra shook her head, taken aback by his reaction. "I am. I thought you would be happy at this news." She folded her arms over her chest.

He threw his arms up in the air. "You were running for your life three weeks ago and you were carrying my child! My foolishness could have seen me lose both my wife and my firstborn. Of course I cannot believe it. How could you have slept in the woods in your condition?"

Thyra bit her lip to keep from laughing. "I did not know I was with child then, although apparently your grandmother suspected it. I had been too preoccupied to notice I had missed my courses. This must have been the third month I missed them." She put a hand over her belly. There was a small curve there that had not been there before. Thyra still felt like she had enjoyed a few too many meals lately rather than feeling pregnant.

He knelt before her, his hands on either side of her waist, prostrating himself before her.

"I am sorry I have put you in such peril. I promise you and this child to never fail like this again."

"Hush, now. You cannot promise that, but I thank you for your redoubled efforts."

He kissed her belly, where the child was growing inside. Then looked up at her with his head cocked to the side, a grin on his face.

"I hadn't even been aware you had stopped drinking your herbs. Were you planning a little surprise all along?"

She smiled back, nodding. "I learned my lesson though. You don't seem to like surprises very much."

He pressed her hand to his chest. "I swear to you, I am so happy my heart is leaping. Can you feel it?"

"I am glad then."

"I want you to rest now. No more running around. Sit down by the fire while I go have a few words with my grandmother."

Gorm was pacing around the room, looking for things she might need.

She hid her smile behind her hand, trying to not let him see she found his behavior amusing. "Don't say anything. She's been nothing but helpful."

Thyra wasn't sure he heard as he shut the door behind him.

8

"CNUT, YOU ARE TOO YOUNG TO GO CHASING AFTER your brother." Thyra scolded her youngest son.

One hand held the struggling five-year-old by the arm while the other applied salve to his wound. He had fallen from a tree. By some miracle the arm hadn't broken, but he had a huge cut which she had washed of debris and was now working on bandaging.

"Mother, you don't know... he said I couldn't go, but you had said I can spend time with him."

Thyra pinched the bridge of her nose.

For one so young, he was proving to be very cunning already. He loved twisting things around to suit his needs. With a bit of training he would make a great statesman one day. No one could disagree with what he said.

"There is a difference between spending time with him and chasing after him as he goes on his hunting trips. He will be back and I'm sure he will find time to play with you." She tried to placate him, but her son's frown had only deepened.

"Why does he get to go? You don't care if he goes swimming in the lake or jumps from high rocks down into the water."

"Harold is twelve years old. It is a very different thing. If I had it my way, I'd lock you both up in a tower and keep you safe forever."

Cnut puffed out his chest. "One day I'll be twelve. Then you won't be able to stop me."

Thyra finished wrapping the bandage around his arm. "No, I won't. Now why don't you go to watch Halfdan in the armory? Stay out of trouble."

She straightened up. Sometimes she found parenting her two boys harder than riding out in the thick of battle. In many respects, she was a typical Christian Queen, but the realities of her world would make her family back in England blanch. That raid in the first year of her marriage had not been the last.

They had been prepared for some, but still they had been forced to flee into the forest several times when their defences had been overwhelmed. They would regroup and eventually drive out the invaders.

Thyra had picked up a weapon to defend her family more than once. She knew what it meant to run a man through with her blade. At first, she had felt remorse after every death but she had quickly become hardened to it. Dealing out death was just a part of her new reality. It was her or them. She had too much to live for now to hesitate.

Over time, these skirmishes grew less and less frequent as Gorm gained more dominance and built up a reputation as a leader and king. Regular patrols were sent out to keep bandits out of the forests and off the roads. The realm was safer, but she also saw Gorm less as a result.

Thyra watched Cnut run off. This would be a good time as any to go pray at the church before finding Harold to scold him for not looking after his brother.

Her eldest son was just like Gorm in many respects, but he had inherited her fiery ambition. She was proud of him, and now that he was through the usual childhood illnesses that claimed so many innocent lives, she could imagine a great future for him.

Olga had lived to see both her grandsons, and though she always seemed to have favored little Cnut, she told Thyra that she could see that Harold had been touched by the gods. An extraordinary destiny lay before him.

Thyra had seen many children die in their cradles, including her own daughter. She still felt the loss deeply, but life had made her tough. She had to be an impenetrable wall to protect her family and loved ones. She lived in fear that she would not be able to do enough to save them.

The church had grown since the time of Father John. Two priests had been sent, and they were much more suited to the work and life here. Together they had developed a small parish and Thyra arranged for all the niceties, such as altar clothes, chalices, and crucifixes. Such projects brought her joy and she dabbled in many other construction projects and improvements. She always on the lookout for a new building project.

She was kneeling in front of the altar, praying for the souls of her dead parents and the health of her family, when she heard a familiar voice behind her.

"I had an inkling I would find you here."

She crossed herself and turned her head to see her husband leaning against the post by the entranceway, watching her.

"Do you need me?"

"Always." The smile that spread across his face was genuine.

"You mean you haven't tired of me after all these years?"

He seemed to consider it. "You make a good point. Perhaps I should trade you in."

"Gorm!" She was now standing in front of him, hands planted on her waist.

He held his hands up as if to defend himself. "Kidding. No, I wanted to show you something."

She followed him out, their arms intertwined like they were still young lovers.

By the stables were two large bay horses. Thyra looked at them closely. They were like the horses her brothers had ridden in England.

She turned to Gorm. "Where did they come from?"

He smiled, urging her forward. She stroked one of the horse's velvety nose.

"War horses all the way from England. Your brothers oversaw their training himself. I want to breed them with our own hardy horses. I doubt they will enjoy our winters here." He patted the neck of the opposite horse. "They are beauties."

Thyra agreed, mesmerized by their beautiful intelligent faces. "They remind me of home. It's silly to suddenly feel homesick after so long away."

Gorm placed a hand on her shoulder to comfort her. "It is all right to miss your home. How are the boys? I heard Cnut was giving you some trouble."

She chuckled. "When does he not? He means well, but trouble always seems to find him."

"Do you want to go for a ride? How long has it been since we've been out alone together?"

She looked around at the bustle of activity, people walking to and fro on their errands, children playing.

She grinned at last. "Let's sneak away before anyone notices."

They rode out the city gates and then urged the horses forward into a canter. Faster and faster they rode, the countryside becoming a blur. Eventually, they stopped on a hill overlooking a grassy plain where sheep and goats were grazing.

They sat down in the field side by side, feeling the cool wind hitting their faces. Thyra leaned her head on Gorm's shoulder.

"What did you want to talk to me about? I know you didn't drag me out here just to have a tumble in a field."

His booming laugh echoed around them. "I always forget how perceptive you are." He tapped her nose before placing a kiss on her lips. "This will be a tough year."

"But the wise man predicted a good harvest."

"Don't interrupt me." He took a deep breath. "Jarl Ulf has died, leaving his land divided and leaderless. It is an opportunity for me. If I move fast enough, before anyone else snatches power, I will have gained us more land and yet another trading passageway."

Thyra frowned but waited for him to continue.

"It is not just for myself that I want this, but if I can somehow establish another kingdom, then Cnut will have an inheritance to call his own as well. I would not want him to feel he was left with nothing. Nor for him to have resentment toward his brother."

"You are a rare man to think of such problems. If you think it is a good idea, then you must do what you think is best." Thyra looked back over the field where the sheep were bleating, mentally preparing herself for the coming separation. If he left, she would not see him for a season at least.

"Well, I would go north if I knew my southern borders were protected."

He was looking at her so intently that he didn't even need to voice his concern.

"My love... I will watch over your lands when you are gone. Is that what you wanted to ask me? Of course I will."

"I am afraid that my scouts are reporting that the Germans are gathering in larger numbers. Raids over the border have increased, and I got nowhere negotiating with the German lord."

"So?"

"What do you think can be done? Is it worth the risk of me going north to leave you here undefended?"

She threw him a smile. "I am not some weak-hearted woman afraid of a challenge. I would have you go north. I will deal with the Germans, and I won't wait for them to attack. I am tired of them always crossing over into our lands. I will keep them out just as Emperor Hadrian kept out the Scots in England."

He furrowed his brows. "Who?"

"He was an old Roman Emperor. He ruled a nation larger than we could even conceive. He built a wall to separate his nation from theirs. To help defend his lands. I will do the same at the southern border. The Danevirke has been worn away by time, but it can be rebuilt and fortified. Once the work is done it, will make it harder for the Germans to maintain supply lines to their armies or send small raiding parties. Even crossing it will be harder. Of course, this cannot be done within a week. But...in any case, what do you think of my plan?"

"I think you are a crazy woman with wild ideas," Gorm said, wrapping an arm around her. "If you can find the people for this, then I would leave with an easy heart, knowing my kingdom is in good hands."

It was easier to plan and dream on that hill than it was to see it put into action. Figuring out the logistics would be the toughest part. Thyra worked hard organizing teams of workers to begin the fortifications. Trees were cut down and shaped into stakes; stones and walls would have to be built. They started to work on it closest to the city of Haithabu, so it could easily be defended if necessary. Out of her own pocket as queen, Thyra hired men to patrol the area to keep troublemakers out and the workers protected.

They had finished a quarter of the wall, with ditches, building up the existing structures and even building an archer tower, when Gorm decided he could wait no longer. He would travel north to try to expand his kingdom.

"Take care, my princess," he said tenderly, their heads pressed together, as though they wanted to drink each other in. "Keep our lands and sons safe."

Thyra sighed, not even bothering to correct him. "Princess" had always been his pet name for her. "I look forward to our reunion. May Odin bless your journey and God keep you safe for me." Her words were heartfelt. He kissed her again and laid a hand on each of their sons' heads. "Be well, my sons."

They were all solemn as they watched Gorm mount his horse and ride out, his company of men following suit.

Life went on. Thyra was always on edge, expecting to hear word of attack at any moment. She slept with a sword at her bedside and her horse was ready to ride out. She had messengers prepared with instructions to ride out to implore all the local lords to come out with their armies to defend Denmark if they were attacked.

Harold walked around the town with an axe hanging

from his belt as if he had taken it upon himself to defend them all. The little lord— that's what everyone called him.

Cnut, meanwhile, seemed to have attached himself to her skirts as though he felt something bad was coming, but he didn't know what.

It happened in the middle of the third week of Gorm's departure. The alarm was raised in the city as a messenger wearing a travel-stained cloak came riding up through the streets of Jelling to warn Thyra of the coming attackers.

At a time like this, she wished Olaf was still here. She gritted her teeth and drew her sword from its hiding place. Her husband had warned her this might come. She had prepared as best she could.

Her heart beat wildly in her chest. She was eager to prove her mettle.

They would gather up a small party and go out to meet these invaders.

A mere few hours later, she had kissed her children and mounted her own horse as she instructed Cnut not to cry. Harold was too old for tears, but he too seemed distraught at her leaving.

She would not shed a tear. She was certain she would return. There was no room for failure or doubt as she led her troop of Danish warriors out to meet the Germans.

Thyra's face was a mask of cool stone. Impassible. Unrelenting.

"For Odin!" she shouted, her fist held up in the air. The returning shouts came over her like a wave, sending the blood in her veins racing. What army could cut them down? What army could bring down the might of Denmark?

Thyra's eyes locked on Harold's; she was proud of his unyielding stance. This was Denmark's future.

She looked away, scanning the faces of her men one last time.

Many might be dining in Valhalla tonight, but their deaths would not be in vain. They would never be defeated. She would not let them be.

AUTHOR'S NOTE

Little is known about Thyra, queen and the "Pride of Denmark." Upon her death Jelling stones were raised in her honor, and they can still be seen today. Even her origin is disputed, as her parentage is not known. Some believe she may have been a noble Englishwoman. For this work of fiction, I have her being one of many English princesses, and daughter of King Ecbert. Myths around her accomplishments exist, and I have incorporated them into this story, including the facts that she led out armies to defend her lands and fortified the Danevirke.

Her son Harold became known as Bluetooth. He became king of Norway as well as Denmark. Bluetooth wireless technology was named after him since it would unite devices the way he had united the tribes of Denmark into a single kingdom. Fun fact, the logo consists of his Nordic initials, H and B.

PREVIEW: JOAN

Love, turmoil, and war. This is the story of Joan de Geneville, wife to one of England's most infamous traitors: Roger Mortimer. After the death of her father in

1292, Joan becomes one of the greatest English heiresses of her generation.

Chapter 1
1292

"Your father is dead." The words were spoken with a firm voice and carried a finality about them that left the six-year-old Joan gaping at her mother.

The little girl felt her eyes well up with tears and she trembled, trying to keep them at bay. Her mother seemed to approve of this and softened for a moment.

"He loved you very much. But now there is important work to be done. Your grandfather will arrive within the week to make the necessary arrangements for the funeral. This affects you most of all as your father's sole heir."

The child blinked in confusion.

"You will inherit everything that is not set aside for your sisters. Does that not please you?"

Joan nodded, even though she still did not quite grasp the importance of the situation.

"Nurse, take Lady Joan to her room and see that she gets a good night's rest."

Nurse Milly, who was standing off to the side, rushed forward and led the little child away.

Alone once more, Jeanne paced the length of the solar. Her mind was churning with all that had to be done. Arrangements would have to be made. Joan stood to become one of the wealthiest heiresses in England. If

Jeanne had her way, with her daughter's good breeding and wealth, an excellent alliance could be formed.

As her mother, Jeanne would also benefit, as she could now live independently and in the lap of luxury, provided that Joan's grandfather allowed her to retain wardship over her own daughter.

She bit her lip at the thought.

The old man was always kindhearted, and with their good relationship she did not see how he could refuse her this request. After all, she had managed the family estates now for nearly five years on her own and proved to be quite successful at it.

Still, Jeanne could not help but worry over her own future. At the age of forty-one, she only had her illustrious family name to recommend her. No one would want a dried-up old spinster. But after a life of disappointment at the hands of men, she looked forward to the prospect of independence.

Meanwhile, in her rooms, Joan, as the elder sister, gathered her siblings around her and told them the news. Neither of them had any recollection of their father, so they did not feel the pang of loss that Joan did.

They were also too young to understand the gravity of death.

Regardless, Joan, acting as their leader, commanded that they should be very sad and that tomorrow they would pick flowers for their father. Beatrice, who could barely walk, gurgled happily.

The nursemaids watching them shook their heads at their childish innocence, but it was not their place to comment. They also watched Joan with particular sadness and jealousy. She would be inheriting riches beyond their dreams, but she would also be fought over by hungry suitors. No doubt Joan would be pushed into an early marriage.

Within the week Baron de Geneville arrived with his retinue at Ludlow.

The house had already gone into mourning and a dour mood had settled over the place. Despite this, there was an efficient harmony to the household that de Geneville appreciated. His daughter-in-law proved to have a good head on her shoulders.

He was greeted in the great hall by a blazing fire. Lady Jeanne stood to greet him, her ladies and three daughters trailing behind her.

"Welcome, Father." She curtsied low.

He kissed her cheeks in familial affection. "I am sorry to see you in such sad times. But to be honest, my son had little more than wool between his ears, and so it is no great loss to our house."

Jeanne did not reply but gave him a soft smile.

"And these young ladies must be my granddaughters." He peered at the trio, studying them. He lingered on the eldest, Joan, with her green eyes. She seemed small for her age, dressed in a formal black gown and cap, but she looked promising enough.

A small nudge from their mother reminded the two oldest girls to curtsy, albeit clumsily, to their grandfather and introduce themselves.

"You must be hungry after your long journey. I have

arranged for a light meal of pheasant and sweetmeats to be prepared in your honor."

"Gracious as ever. My men will eat here in the great hall, but I hope you will do me the honor of dining with me in private, as we have much to discuss."

Jeanne nodded.

They retreated to the solar, accompanied by a footman and a maidservant to wait upon them.

As they walked, Sir Geoffrey de Geneville noted the improvements made to Ludlow. It had been almost a decade since he had last stepped inside the house, and he was pleasantly surprised by what he saw. It had clearly been maintained well and tastefully decorated without being overly extravagant.

There were new tapestries hanging on the walls and a sweet scent of lavender seemed to linger in the air.

Sometimes he wondered at that son of his, who had proved to be such a disappointment. Peter had squandered his wealth and position. He spent his life pursuing pleasure rather than taking up any responsibility or showing any sort of ambition—a sin in Geoffrey's eyes.

There was no one to blame but his mother, who had spoiled him as a child. Even in adulthood, she had rewarded his laziness by bestowing upon him all of her English holdings.

Having finally reached the solar, he claimed the seat nearest to the fire.

At the age of sixty-six, he was finally starting to show his age. Most of his fellow peers had long since passed away, while until recently he had still been going strong.

The pair ate in silence for several moments. Both trying to determine the measure of the other.

"Would you like some more wine?" Jeanne inquired, breaking the silence.

"No. I have whetted my appetite enough. I feel both of us are ready to speak of more important matters." He took a moment to collect his thoughts. "My son's death came at an untimely moment. He left us without a proper heir. Even his eldest daughter is barely six—she is healthy, isn't she?"

"Yes, she was always the picture of health." Jeanne reassured him.

Her father-in-law nodded his approval and continued. "At least there will be time to groom her properly and arrange an appropriate betrothal for her." He stroked his gray beard, thinking of potential families.

"And what of her wardship?"

Geoffrey felt the tension rise in the room. It was uncommon for the mother to retain custody of her children after the death of the father, but he was too old to think of rearing children and had his own business to attend to in Ireland. He could trust no other to keep the family fortunes and lands intact.

"I spoke with my lady-wife Matilda on the matter." He paused again. "We think you ought to retain custody of the children. Of course, changes will have to be made. Matilda feels Joan should have a tutor for Latin and history. As our heir it is important she is somewhat educated, as unconventional as it may be."

"Thank you, sir." Jeanne took his hands in hers and kissed them in gratitude.

"There are other arrangements to be made for the other girls."

"Sir?"

"They should enter the nunnery. That way they will not be able to contest any claim on Joan's land in the future."

"I assure you I would not let them." The thought of resigning her younger daughters to a nunnery did not appeal to her.

"I do not doubt your daughters, but their future husbands. Men are greedy by nature. I will not be swayed in this matter." He stood firm.

"Of course, milord." Jeanne acquiesced, hiding her disappointment by focusing on the happier news.

"I ride for London in a fortnight. When I return I hope to have made the arrangements in regards to Joan's future." He stood, wiping his hands on a napkin. "Your hospitality has been happily received, but now I am afraid I must retire for the night. My old bones cannot handle traveling as well as they used to. We shall speak more in the days to come."

Jeanne thanked him once more and bid him good night.

Before she retired, she went to see her children.

She crept into their room, as they were fast asleep already.

They looked so angelic. She placed a hand on Joan's head, stroking her soft dark hair. There would be so much pressure put on her. And her sisters would no doubt in their jealousy grow to hate her. But for now they were still children and could enjoy each other's company.

In an uncharacteristic show of motherly affection, Jeanne leaned over each of them and kissed their brows.

Printed in Great Britain
by Amazon